Unexpected

by

Janice Cole Hopkins

Janice Cole Hopkins

Other Books by Janice Cole Hopkins

For I know the thoughts that I think toward you, saith the LORD, thoughts of peace, and not of evil, to give you an expected end.

- Jeremiah 29:11-

Chapter One: An Unexpected Offer

Oakboro, North Carolina, June 30, 1961

Oliver Hartsell moved his ladder to the next window and stopped to wipe the sweat from his face before climbing it again. Mr. Austin had hired him to replace two cracked windowpanes, but Mr. Little, his boss at the hardware, hadn't told him until after lunch.

He maneuvered the sashes, so he could better reach the broken glass. He couldn't understand why Mr. Austin didn't have central air conditioning. Oliver's family couldn't afford it, but the Austins seemed to have enough money.

"You are what!" He heard Mr. Austin yell. "Were you forced?"

"No, Daddy." Marie wavered as if she were about to cry.

Why you are nothing but a w...."

"Gunther, don't," his wife cut in. "There's no need for name-calling. It won't help a thing."

"No, it won't help anything." Marie tried to sound resolved, but her voice still trembled.

Oliver's heart constricted for her. He'd always liked Marie. She was smart, sweet, kind to everyone, and pretty. In fact, he liked her a lot – too much likely if the truth be told.

"I can't believe it," Mrs. Austin said. "Are you sure?"

"I went to see Dr. McCloud yesterday."

Oliver clutched the ladder tightly to keep from falling off. Was Marie seriously sick? It sounded like something terrible.

"When are you due?" her mother asked.

"Sometime in February the best we can figure."

Due in February. Was Marie expecting a baby? Oliver almost did fall off the ladder. When he recovered, he repositioned on the ladder, so he could see into the room. He needed to see Marie's face. She sat on the sofa by herself, looking down at her hands in her lap.

Mrs. Austin sat in a chair. "Who's the father? Have you told him? Will he marry you?"

"I told him, and he says he's not ready for marriage and a family yet." Big tears rolled out of Marie's eyes."

Mr. Austin started pacing the floor. "Best get an abortion, then."

Marie straightened, and her blue eyes grew large. "I will not get an abortion."

Oliver closed his eyes for a second. Good for her. An abortion certainly wouldn't be the answer."

"I agree with Marie on that." Mrs. Austin twisted her apron and looked to see how her husband would react to her disagreeing with him. "Maybe we could send her away to stay with a relative and she could give the baby up for adoption. That way no one here would know."

Mr. Austin gave his wife a withering look but said nothing to her about contradicting him. "I guess that might work."

"I-I want to keep my baby." Marie's voice cracked as she pleaded.

"You will not!" Mr. Austin yelled again. "You'll be a ruined woman, and no one would ever want to marry you. You do want a husband and a family, don't you?"

Marie nodded, the movement causing more tears to fall from her tear-stained face. She looked so broken Oliver wanted to cry for her.

He leaned his head through the open window. "I'll marry her."

Every head turned to him. Marie turned red, Mrs. Austin looked wide-eyed, and Mr. Austin spoke. "I forgot you were out there somewhere, Oliver. What did you say?"

Oliver cleared his throat. What had he done? He never spoke up boldly like this, but he didn't regret it. "I said I would be willing to marry Marie."

Although he'd spoken out before he thought, what he said was true, nonetheless. He and Marie had been lab partners their sophomore year, and he had fallen for her. Yet, he could never get up the courage to ask her out because he knew she would never accept a date with him. She was popular, and he wasn't. He had watched her often, however, and his feelings had grown.

Everyone stayed silent for much too long, and Oliver felt his face growing hotter than ever. Surely it hadn't turned red. Men shouldn't blush.

"That might be a solution I'd never thought of." Mr. Austin looked from his daughter to his wife.

Mrs. Austin nodded her approval. "If we can hurry the wedding along and they marry before Marie starts showing, that should work."

"I don't want to marry anyone but Der…." Marie slammed her hand over her mouth.

Mr. Austin's face almost steamed in anger. "Derrick Tucker! I'll kill the boy!"

"No, Daddy. That won't change the fact that I'm going to have a baby. It would just get you in a lot of trouble."

Mr. Austin seemed to be turning something over in his mind. "You got pregnant on that prom night, didn't you? I knew I shouldn't have let you go. You came in two hours after I told you to be home, too."

Marie didn't answer, but she didn't need to. Oliver's stomach rolled over at the thought. He shook his head to get rid of the image of Marie being so beautiful dressed in her formal gown and then removing it all for Derrick.

"You sure you want to do this?" Mr. Austin asked him. "Get down from there and come on in here so we can talk about it.

Oliver did as he was told. Marie gave him a brief glance as he walked into the room and then turned her gaze back to her hands. He wished she would look him in the eyes, so he might know what she was thinking. But then, she'd already indicated that she wanted to marry Derrick. His stomach threatened to throw up his lunch. The bologna sandwich he'd eaten hadn't settled well, and this situation with so much attention now on him continued to kick it around.

"Marrying Oliver would be the best thing," Mrs. Austin told Marie.

"It's the only choice she has if she wants to keep the baby," Mr. Austin added. "You hear me, girl?"

Marie nodded. Oliver didn't know if she was agreeing to marry him or if she simply acknowledged she had heard her father. He had never dreamed he would propose to a woman this way.

Mr. Austin looked at his wife. "When should we plan this?"

"The sooner the better." She looked at Oliver. "If Oliver and she go to the Fourth of July celebration together, and everyone sees them holding hands there, it shouldn't be a big shock when they get married about two or three weeks later."

Mr. Austin nodded his approval. "Good idea. I want them wed before the end of July. I'll talk to the preacher. You and Marie plan the rest." He turned to Oliver. "You can take care of getting the license. Do you need some money?"

Oliver bit back his embarrassment. "No, sir. I have some money." Not much, he thought, but enough to pay for the license, and he wanted to pay his part and provide for Marie.

"You can get your tux, too," Mrs. Austin said.

Marie looked up. "I don't want a formal wedding with a wedding gown and all that. I'll just wear a dress and Oliver can wear a suit."

She did plan to marry him then. He breathed a sigh of relief.

"That's probably for the best," Mr. Austin agreed. "It will take less time to get everything organized, cause less fuss, and cost less money in the bargain."

"Have you told anyone else about this?" Mrs. Austin asked Marie.

"No. Just Derrick, Dr. McCloud and his nurse, you, and now Oliver know."

Mr. Austin looked at his daughter. "Good. Keep it that way. If you tell any of your friends, it's bound to get out."

He turned to Oliver. "Go on and get your job done." He shifted to see Marie. "And you go to your room and think about your sins until it's time to help your mother with supper."

Oliver had hoped for a chance to talk with Marie alone, but he did what Mr. Austin said. Maybe he could have a talk with his fiancée after he finished with the glass.

For once, Marie was glad to be sent to her room. She closed the door and took a deep breath, but it didn't help. She took a few steps and fell onto the bed, burying her face in the pillow to muffle the sound.

She didn't know how long she lay there, releasing the gut-wrenching sobs she had managed to hold back while talking with her parents. She had dreaded telling them about the baby so much that she almost didn't. If Derrick had just married her, she wouldn't have had to. But now she had little choice. She had no money and no way to leave. She thought about running away and living on the streets in some city, but she didn't want that type of lifestyle for her or her baby. Derrick offered to pay for an abortion but nothing more.

She knew telling her parents would be bad, and it was, but it would have been much worse if Oliver had not been there. His presence prevented her father from going berserk.

Oliver. She couldn't believe that he'd offered to marry her. What in the world had possessed him to do that? Did he feel that sorry for her? She didn't want his pity. Would he regret the offer after he'd had time to consider it? Maybe he would back out, and that would suit her just fine. She didn't want to marry Oliver Hartsell.

But if he did back out, what would she do? Could her father force her to have an abortion or give her baby up for adoption, even though she was eighteen? She had no doubt he would try.

Despite the fact that he had disappointed her, she still loved Derrick. One didn't cut real love off like a water faucet. Why wouldn't he marry her? On his prom night, he'd indicated they had a future together. She knew she shouldn't have done what she did, but his kisses and touches had made her lose all thought of anything else, and she'd wanted what he wanted – fool that she was.

She rubbed her stomach. At least she'd get to keep her baby if she married Oliver. He was a nice enough guy, but she would never have chosen him for a husband. He had been way too quiet and shy in school, and the hecklers had found him an easy target.

If they hadn't been lab partners in biology class, she wouldn't have known him at all.

She'd found him gentle and kind. He had always done the messy tasks or the parts that required manual skill, leaving her to write up the experiments and any steps she particularly wanted to do. They had talked very little and never chatted like friends, but it had been a surprisingly comfortable silence. She had liked him well enough at the time, but she certainly didn't love him.

Suddenly, thoughts of sleeping with him as husband and wife made her cringe. Could she do it? She felt sure he would expect it; any man would. Maybe she could close her eyes and imagine he was Derrick. As repugnant as that made her feel, it might be the only way she could endure it.

She took a deep breath and let it out, hoping to dispel unwanted thoughts, but it came out more like a shudder. What a mess she had gotten herself into. How she wished she could go back and change things, but she couldn't. She felt soiled, degraded, and rejected. She had never been good enough for Father, and apparently, she wasn't good enough for Derrick either.

The one good thing about marrying Oliver, he would make a great father if he'd accept another man's child. She didn't think he would mistreat her, either. She guessed her situation could be worse, but not by much. If only she could convince Derrick to marry her.

"Marie, telephone!" her mother called from the bottom of the steps.

Marie sat up and tried to shake off the sleep. She must have dozed off. Maybe it was Derrick calling. She hurried to see.

"Don't you be on that phone all day," her father groused. "Just because you're getting married doesn't mean the same rules don't apply."

"Hello,"

"Hello, Marie. Th-this is Oliver."

"Yes?" She tried to hide the disappointment in her voice, but she didn't know if she succeeded.

"Uh, your mother said you were resting when I left, but I thought we needed to talk. About things," he added when she didn't respond.

She wanted to tell him he had disturbed that rest, but she didn't. "All right." She guessed he was right, but she didn't want to talk right now. Would he ask her about Derrick?

"Could I see you tonight? We could go somewhere, even get some supper if you'd like."

"I'm exhausted, Oliver. Could we make it some other time?"

"Of course." His voice softened. "I-I should have realized this has been an emotional, draining time for you. What about tomorrow?"

She suddenly recognized how nervous and

unsure he sounded. This must be hard for him, too. After all, they were practically strangers. "Okay."

"I usually get off work around five. I'll pick you up at six if that's all right."

"That would be fine."

"Where would you like to go?"

"Why don't we plan to eat here first?" She knew Oliver probably had to watch his money. "I always help with the cooking anyway. Then we can go somewhere to talk."

"All right. I'll see you tomorrow, then."

"Oliver's coming for supper tomorrow," she informed her parents after she hung up the phone.

"Great, now I get to feed another mouth," her father complained. "Don't think I'll be supporting that baby, either. I know how much money infants take."

Was that the reason she had been an only child? Had her father been too stingy to want more children? But her mother had always said she couldn't have any more.

She wanted to go back to her room, crawl into bed, and go back to sleep, but she trudged into the kitchen instead. Her mother would expect her to help with supper. She usually did most of the cooking under her mother's supervision to make sure she did things to suit her father.

She dreaded seeing Oliver tomorrow. She didn't want to start the next phase of her life, one that would see her married to a man she didn't love or want.

Chapter Two: An Unexpected Proposal

Things didn't go well for Oliver the next day. He couldn't get his mind off Marie, and he made more mistakes than he ever had.

"What's wrong with you, son?" Mr. Little finally asked.

"I don't know, sir. I guess I'm just having a bad day." He hadn't told anyone about marrying Marie yet, not even his parents, but he planned to tell them soon. He'd have to. They would be surprised, even shocked, but he felt sure they would support him. He just didn't want them to think badly of Marie.

Mr. Little almost looked amused. "Well, don't make it a habit."

Oliver jerked to attention. He had been lost in his own thoughts.

Mr. Little laughed. "You looked a million miles away. Must be some girl on your mind. That's about the only thing that makes a fellow act like that."

Oliver didn't say anything, but Mr. Little was used to him not saying much. Everyone, except his family, knew him to be quiet and shy.

That's one thing he dreaded about talking with Marie tonight. It would make him uncomfortable, but it had to be done. They needed to make plans.

He resolved to treat Marie more like his family.

If he didn't let her get to know him, how would she ever come to care for him? He knew she didn't love him yet, but he would treat her so well she would have to come to love him.

Derrick was a fool. Oliver couldn't imagine why the guy wouldn't want to marry Marie and give their baby his name, but Oliver would show Marie what a responsible, caring man could be like. He would win her heart.

Although his proposal had been impulsive and without thought, he still felt that he had done the right thing. Marrying Marie felt right, almost as if God had been directing him.

He sighed. Marrying Marie was a dream come true – a secret dream that he'd never imagined would come true. He could hardly believe his good fortune, but then God often showered unexpected blessings on his children.

He just hoped Marie would come to see him as a blessing. He instinctively knew his feelings for her were much stronger than hers for him. But she had been friendly and kind when they were lab partners, and she'd always smiled at him when they passed in the hall, so at least she liked him. That was more than he could say of most of their classmates.

Oliver had a vicious cycle going on. The quieter he became the more others his age picked on him, and the more they picked on him the quieter he became. He would not wish the curse of being this shy on anyone. He would try harder to overcome some of it for Marie, especially when he was with her.

His thoughts turned to the baby. Although he would have liked for the situation to be different, he would accept the child as his. He would make sure it had everything it needed, including lots of love. After all, it was Marie's child, and therefore it would be easy for him to love.

That's one thing his family had been rich on. They had never had a lot of material possessions or money, but they had each other and knew they were loved. Between God's love and his family's, he felt like he had more than many people did.

And he would shower Marie and the baby with as much love as he had. The way her parents had talked to her angered him. Yes, she needed to be shown love. Her father seemed particularly cold and uncaring about her feelings. Just the thought of it made his heart twist into a knot. He would do everything he could to give her a good life, a happy one.

Oliver hurried home, showered, and changed clothes. He didn't put on church clothes for that might be overdoing things, but he dressed in his nicest jeans and shirt.

He borrowed his dad's old truck. They had been sharing it since Oliver got his driver's license. That had become more difficult when Oliver started working, but his father worked on the farm, and Oliver usually took the truck, unless his father needed it that day. Then, his father would drop him off and pick him up. On those days, he took Mr. Little's vehicle if he needed to go out on a job.

He looked at the old Ford. It had a few dents and had faded some over the years, but the forest green paint kept some of the rust spots from showing so much. At least he tried to keep it cleaned up. He wished he had something better for Marie to ride in, but he didn't.

Derrick had a flashy red Corvette if he remembered correctly. He would never be able to compete with him on most things. But he wanted to love and take care of Marie and the baby, and he hoped that would be worth more than any material possessions.

His heart started beating irregularly as he approached the Austin's porch. He needed to be above approach with them all. Just the thoughts of them watching him eat and needing to make conversation sent game roosters pecking at his stomach. He tried to swallow, but his mouth and throat were too dry.

The front door stood open, but the screen door was closed. His knock sounded faint. Had anyone heard it?

Marie came to the door wiping her hands on a kitchen towel. She held the door open, "Come on in, Oliver. You're right on time."

He liked the sound of her calling his name, but she didn't smile. Was she as uncomfortable with tonight as he was? Had her parents made it hard on her today?

"Follow me. I'll stick my head in the den to tell Daddy that supper's ready, and then we'll go to the dining room.

Oliver nodded and followed Marie. The Austins had a living room and den and a kitchen and dining room with only three of them in the family. His family's house only had a living room and a kitchen for eight people. He felt more out of his league all the time.

Oliver held Marie's chair for her to be seated at the table before taking the place they'd indicated for him and sitting beside her. Mr. Austin's hard eyes stared at him, but Oliver ignored the man. He had gotten good at ignoring disapproving people over the years.

Marie looked especially pretty tonight in a white sundress with black polka dots. When he pushed her up, his face came close to her head, and she smelled good, too – something fresh and lightly floral like flowers after a rain shower.

Had she dressed special for him? The thought

almost made him smile. Almost.

"I've been thinking." Mr. Austin spoke with his mouth full after they had all started eating. "I have no intentions of supporting y'all once you're married. A man ought not to get married if he can't support his family."

"I agree, Mr. Austin. I have every intention of taking care of Marie and our baby."

That stopped the man. He finished chewing his bite and swallowed. "But I do have a house of sorts that used to belong to my grandparents. It's small, but it is closer to town and should be fine for a young couple starting out."

"But that's nothing but a shack?" Marie looked at her father in disbelief.

"Be that as it may, the rent will be cheap, and I'm sure Oliver can fix it up nice enough. After all, I hear he's a pretty good carpenter."

Oliver started to agree, but Marie cut him off. "So, you plan to charge rent and still have Oliver renovate the place? That doesn't sound fair. If we're going to remodel, that should be enough."

Mr. Austin's stare cut into Marie, saying things he didn't voice, but she held her chin up and stared right back. Oliver had a feeling she wouldn't get away with her resolve had he not been present as their guest.

"Oh, all right," Mr. Austin finally said, "but you'll need to furnish your own materials. The place isn't doing me any good just sitting there, and I can't rent it anymore in its condition. But I do expect to see some steady progress made." His gaze swung to Oliver.

"I will work on it as much as I can," he agreed. "My job will have to come first, though."

"I can understand that," Mr. Austin surprised him by saying. "You'll have plenty of expenses with setting up a household and a youngin' on the way."

The fried chicken and garden vegetables he'd been eating suddenly turned to lead in his stomach. He'd been worrying about those things all day. If he had known he'd be getting married this summer, he would have saved more of his money instead of giving most of it to his parents to help ends meet.

"And we get to live there as long as we want, even after the repairs are finished." Marie continued with her bargaining.

"Now I don't know about that. I might need to charge rent sometime down the line."

"Then you plan to fix up the place even if we don't move in and do it?" Marie asked.

"Wel-l, no." Mr. Austin rubbed his chin.

"Then it would be better if Oliver and I lived in it instead of just letting the house fall in."

"Oh, all right, but don't think you can keep getting your way."

"Of course not." Marie looked away, as though

she had pushed as far as she dared.

As everyone stood to leave the table, Oliver turned to Marie. "Shall we go for a drive?"

"I may need to help Mama with the dishes first?" She looked at her mother.

"No, that's okay. You go ahead. I can take care of the clean-up tonight."

"Thanks, Mama." Marie gave her mother a weak smile.

Oliver wished she would smile more often. She had a beautiful one. He thanked the Austins for having him over and told Mrs. Austin how much he enjoyed the food.

"Marie cooked most of it," the older woman told him.

Oliver tried to hide his surprise. He had assumed Marie didn't do much of the work and that she had been pampered as an only child. He now knew differently after just two short visits here, but he liked the fact that she could cook and cook so well.

As they started out, he heard her daddy turn on the television. The news blasted updates on the Vietnam War.

Marie turned to Oliver. "Daddy is worried that the war is going to escalate. I hope not."

He gave an uncomfortable smile. "I do, too. But if things get worse, I may be exempt because I have flat feet and a slight heart mummer. It's something I developed not long after birth, but it's never affected me.

As they walked to Oliver's truck side by side, she recalled how worried Derrick had been that he'd be drafted. She didn't know why the fact that Oliver might be ineligible cause her such happiness, but it did.

He opened the door on the passenger's side for her and she slid in. Derrick had tended to get in the driver's seat first and reach across to flick her door open.

The truck was old, but it looked immaculately clean, and it started without a problem. She sat close to the door, but not so far from Oliver that it would look odd.

"I wish I had a better vehicle for us, but this is our only family vehicle." Oliver's face turned a little pink.

Had she been looking at the truck too much? Did he think she would think less of him for his farm truck?

"As long as it gets us where we need to be, that's what matters." She could tell her comment pleased him, but she decided to change the subject. "Where are we going?"

There's a pond down in the field on our property. It's far enough from the house that no one should bother us, and there's a separate dirt road that goes down to it, so we can drive all the way.

"That sounds good." And this way she wouldn't see anyone that might question her. Her friends were going to flip out when they saw her with Oliver, much less learn she planned to marry him.

They sat in a silence that made her uncomfortable, and she wanted to say something. "Father gave into me on my great-grandparent's house easier than I thought he would."

Oliver glanced her way and grinned. "You were quite the negotiator. I should take you with me when we go to buy a car. I'm proud of you."

Marie set back in the seat, almost as if some invisible force had pushed her. Had anyone ever said they were proud of her? If so, she couldn't remember when.

When they pulled off the paved road and headed down the dirt road, the ride became bumpy and sometimes jolting. Oliver slowed the truck to a crawl.

"This isn't too much for you, is it?" His face filled with concern.

She paused to wonder why that question but then realized he asked because she was expecting.

"No, I'm fine."

They pulled up to a pasture, and Oliver got out to open the gate. He came back, drove the truck through, and then went back and closed the gate. Maybe she should have offered to get the gate, but she hadn't thought of it in time.

When he parked the truck, he hurried around to open her door and help her out. His mama had raised him right.

He led her to a bench beside the pond and then sat down beside her – too close to suit her, but she said nothing. Since it got dark so much later in the summer, she could still see clearly, and she looked around. A few cattle grazed in the distance, and frogs occasionally croaked in the pond. The lush, green grass was speckled with clover and a few wildflowers. "This is pretty. How much property does your family own?"

"About a hundred and fifty acres. There used to be two hundred, but we've had to sell some. Dad hates doing that and tries to avoid it if at all possible. He says. if he has to sell any more, he won't have enough to make a living farming."

"I'm surprised you aren't helping him on the farm full-time."

"My brothers do some of the work, and I help out a lot, but my job at the hardware has brought in extra cash that we needed. Besides, I like carpentry, although what I would really like to be doing is building furniture, and Mr. Little lets me take repair jobs on the side."

A thought crossed Marie's mind. "Did you build this bench?" She ran her hand over the smooth slats.

"I did. It's nice to have for fishing, too."

"I'd like to come fishing sometime. I haven't fished much, but I liked it when I tried."

He gave her an off-center grin. "I think that can be arranged." Then he turned serious and cleared his throat.

Uh-oh, here it came. He must be getting ready to ask her about Derrick.

"Marie, I want to talk about us. This all happened so fast I don't think you've had much of a say in matters." He picked up her hand and held it gently in his. She wanted to jerk it away, but she didn't. "I want you to have a say. Marie, would you do me the honor of being my wife? The choice is yours."

Her surprise must have shown because he gave her a tender smile. She hadn't expected him to actually propose tonight. But if the choice were really hers, she'd say no. However, the baby needed both a father and a mother without an irreparable reputation. Even if she could weather the fallout from being an unwed mother, and that was a big "if," she needed to consider what would be best for the baby.

She blinked, and as Oliver came into focus again, she saw the panic on his face. Did he really want to marry her that much? "If you are willing, I am, but I don't want you to feel obligated. I know you said you would marry me on the spur-of-the-moment. If you feel differently now, I'll understand."

"I haven't changed my mind," he answered quickly. "Is that a yes you'll marry me?"

She couldn't help but smile at the happy lilt to his voice. "Yes, I'll marry you."

He lifted her hand to his lips like the hero from an old-fashioned novel. She started to cringe, but when his lips touched her hand, the kiss didn't feel that bad. Yet, she couldn't help but be thankful that he hadn't given her a real one on the lips. She knew she wasn't ready for that yet.

"Why did you do it, Oliver?" She had to ask.

"Do what?"

"Say that you would marry me."

"I couldn't stand to hear your father yelling at you and start to call you names, and I've always liked you. I feel as if I'm the most blessed man on earth to get to marry you."

He sounded so sincere she couldn't doubt him. But what did "like her" mean? The way he said it made her think he might mean more. But, how could he? They had never dated. In fact, they had never been around each other much except for some classes where they sat on opposite sides of the room.

Biology lab had been the one exception, but he had been so shy, they hadn't talked much more than about the assignment. He couldn't know her, and she certainly didn't know him. She didn't ask any further questions about it, however. She might not want to hear his answer.

Chapter Three: The Unexpected Engagement

Oliver pulled a small black velvet-covered box from his pocket. He opened it and presented Marie with a diamond ring. She hadn't expected a ring tonight, either.

"It was my grandmother's ring. She wanted me to have it to give to my future wife." He took the ring out of the slot in the box and slipped it on her finger.

The ring fit perfectly, another surprise. Marie looked at the ring. It wasn't big, not over a third of a carat, but she liked the old-fashioned setting.

She looked up at Oliver and saw the worry lines across his forehead. "It is beautiful. Thank you."

His face relaxed. I haven't told my parents yet. Would you like to go to the house with me now to do that?"

"No!" It came out more forcefully than she intended. She calmed her voice. "Let me do that later when they are expecting me. I think it would be better if you told them by yourself first. That way if they say something hurtful, I won't have to hear it."

"Okay. Mom will probably want to have you over for supper then." He gave her hand a reassuring squeeze. "But they won't say anything hurtful. They will be pleased for me because they want me to be happy."

Should she believe him? That seemed so far removed from how her parents had reacted she couldn't help but wonder.

He stood but didn't let go of her hand. "I guess we should be going. I hear some mosquitoes buzzing around, and I don't want them to bite you."

"Yes, I get tired more easily lately, and it's been a long day." And she was ready for this time with Oliver to end. She found it all too confusing. She didn't know how to react to his kindness. Her head told her he would be her husband, and she owed him her allegiance, but her heart fought to keep Derrick there.

He nodded and led her back to his truck. He seemed so solicitous she didn't know what to think. Unwanted tears formed behind her eyes from the uncertainty of it all.

As they started off, she looked at Oliver. He had acted much more normal tonight than she had ever seen him – not so withdrawn and shy. He had talked more, too.

"I'm sorry about what I did." For some reason, she felt she needed to say something about the baby, but now some tears did slide down her face. "I know what I did was wrong, but I still want this baby."

"I think you are doing the right thing in keeping it. It's a part of you, and I will love it because of that.

He or she will be ours."

"Thank you." It's all she could manage before her voice broke. She turned her face toward the door on her side because her tears had started falling faster.

He put his hand on her arm. "It will be all right. We'll make it so."

Could they? Would anything ever be all right again? That would truly be a miracle, but only God could work those, and she had disappointed Him like she had everyone else, including herself. God must surely have turned His back on her now.

"Do you want to go to church with me and the family tomorrow? Then you can eat dinner with us. Mom always cooks a big Sunday dinner.

She sniffed and started to refuse. But maybe going to his church would be better than all the questions she would have to answer at hers if Daddy told Uncle Leonard what she'd done, or folks learned that she was seeing Oliver. At least, Oliver would be there for support if any questions came about why they were together. "Okay."

"Good. We'll pick you up about nine-thirty."

They arrived at her house about that time. Oliver parked the truck, helped her out, and walked her to the door. "I'll see you tomorrow. Sleep well." He leaned over and kissed her cheek."

She partially opened the door but watched him walk to his truck before she went inside. The lightness of his step and the way he moved spoke of happiness. She wished she could feel like that.

Oliver hummed a tune he had heard earlier on the radio as he drove home, glad that the old thing still worked. Tonight had gone well, except for Marie's tears. She hurt over Derrick's betrayal and her parent's harsh reaction, and he couldn't make it go away right now. He could only marry her, treat her special, and love her. Eventually, he hoped that would work to right her world. It had to.

He actually felt good about tonight. He'd been able to talk to Marie without the words hanging in his throat before he got them out, and she'd agreed to marry him without her parents pressuring her.

When he got home, he sat in the truck for a moment to hold tight to the happiness he still felt from being with Marie. Then, he hurried into the house to tell his parents about her and their engagement.

His mother looked up from her mending. "You're looking mighty happy."

"I've got some good news." He moved to the chair across from his parents on the sofa.

"Oh?" His father put down the paper he'd been

reading. Probably a free one because they didn't spend money on the *Stanly News and Press*.

"Marie Austin has agreed to marry me. That's where I've been. I ate supper at her house and proposed down by our pond." His parents didn't need to know all the details now. That could come later.

Both sat frozen in place with their mouths open. He knew they'd be surprised, but shock better described this.

His mother recovered first. "Isn't this rather sudden? What brought this on?"

"I didn't know you knew her or that you'd been dating," his father added.

"I know her from school. We had a lot of classes together, and I got to know her well when we were lab partners in biology. We haven't really dated much, though." None, in fact, until tonight, but he didn't tell them that either.

"Well, I can tell you're thrilled." His mother looked pleased. "I hope you two will be very happy.

His father shook his head. "I knew you'd be getting married someday, but I didn't think it would be this soon. Are you sure you're ready for this, son?"

"Henry, Oliver has always been the most responsible one of our children. He will make a wonderful husband and father. And he's as old as you were when we were married."

His dad looked chastised at his wife's gentle

admonishment. "You're right, Louise. I guess I'm just not ready to see him leave home yet."

"Neither am I, but he needs our support." A wide grin broke across her face. "Besides, we might get to be grandparents before you know it."

His dad smiled, too. Yeah, spoil 'em and then send 'em home."

Oliver cleared his throat, seeing the opening. "That day may be here before you thought."

His mom caught onto what he meant before his father. "She's already expecting?"

Oliver nodded. He hated misleading his parents, but he didn't want them to think the worst of Marie before they got to know her. Besides, the fewer people who knew the truth about the baby's real father, the better for everyone, especially right now.

"I'm surprised at you Oliver." He hoped that wasn't disappointment he saw on his father's face. "But at least you've stepped up and done the right thing in marrying her."

"I'm not at all sorry to be marrying Marie. I've loved her for a long time. Things will work out."

"Do her parents know?" Mom asked.

"Yes. That's likely the only reason they would let her marry me."

"Then they don't know you well. Marie is a blessed woman to get you for a husband. I could think of no better."

"Thanks." His mom had always been his ardent supporter and cheerleader. She was that way with all her children but especially with him.

"Well, I'm going up to bed." Oliver stood. "Is that where everyone else is?"

"They all went upstairs," Dad said, "but I don't know that they're in bed."

"Oh." Oliver turned back around. "I invited Marie to go to church with us tomorrow and eat dinner with us. Will that be all right?

"Of course," Mother responded. "She's part of the family now."

"There's always room for one more," Dad said. "You'll probably need to sit in the bed of the truck with the others and let Marie and your mama ride up front with me, but we'll manage."

Oliver continued upstairs. He and his three brothers slept in one bedroom, and his two sisters slept in the other one. His parents' room was downstairs.

He heard his brother's laughter before he opened the door, but he didn't mind. His excitement over talking with Marie and getting to see her tomorrow kept him from being sleepy and ready to settle down just yet. They could stay up as long as they wanted tonight, and he wouldn't be bothered.

"You shouldn't be going and making decisions like this without asking first," Marie's daddy continued. "You know I don't approve of any other church, except the one your Uncle Leonard preaches at."

"If Oliver's going to be my husband, don't you think I need to get used to trying to please him?" Marie used the one argument she thought her father would agree with. He believed the man should be the head of his household.

"Well, I still don't like it. You aren't married yet, and until you are, you're still part of this family, but I won't stop you this time. Just remember to ask me first when anything else comes up."

Marie nodded. Getting out from under her father's thumb would be one benefit of marriage. From what she'd seen, she didn't think Oliver would be nearly as controlling. Come to think of it, even Derrick seemed more demanding than Oliver.

Marie tried to take one more bite of eggs, but the smell caused her to place her fork back on her plate. She took a bite of dry toast instead. Her stomach had been queasy every morning lately, but thankfully it usually wore off by ten o'clock. She should be okay at church.

She dressed with care, choosing the latest dress she'd made. The sleeveless navy and white gingham dress had a fitted bodice and full skirt. It also had a short, waist-length jacket with three-quarter length sleeves to match.

When she put it on, she noticed it fit a bit snugger than it had when she made it. How long would she be able to wear her clothes? She hated the thought of wearing ugly maternity clothes, but she guessed she needed to get busy making some.

The thoughts of going through all the changes alone scared her so much she almost felt glad she would be marrying Oliver. She would never love him like she did Derrick, but maybe they could become close friends.

Her parents usually left for church early. Her father liked to be one of the first ones there, but today, they waited until the Hartsells pulled up to get her. She guessed her father didn't trust her enough to leave her at the house alone for a few minutes.

Oliver jumped out of the cab and met her in the yard. "Come on, and I'll introduce you to everyone."

He called the names of his brothers and sisters in the back first. Then he led her to the cab, introduced his parents, and helped her into the seat beside his mother. He closed the door, and she heard him climb into the back with the others.

Marie didn't know how he would manage to fit there because it had been full before, but he must have managed. Mr. Hartsell had been watching in the rearview mirror but soon started off, so she assumed Oliver had settled.

Mrs. Hartsell patted her hand. I'm thrilled to have you join our family. I've never seen Oliver so happy."

Marie breathed a little sigh of relief. The woman sounded so sincere and friendly she couldn't help but believe her.

Mrs. Hartsell lowered her voice. "I'm surprised Oliver didn't behave like the Christian gentleman we taught him to be, and I apologize for him wronging you, but at least he's trying to do what's right now. And I'm tickled to death to have a grandchild on the way."

At first, Marie didn't understand what she was saying, but then she finally understood. Oliver had led them to believe the child was his. She could hardly take it in.

She knew she needed to say something in response, and she searched for some truth that would fit. "He's a good man."

Mrs. Hartsell's smile told her that she had chosen well. "He's got a good heart, for sure."

Marie nodded. She could agree with that wholeheartedly. Otherwise, he wouldn't be marrying her and claiming the baby as his own.

They pulled up to the church, and Mr. Hartsell parked the truck. This brick church looked different than the wooden structure she'd always attended. Before she had much time to look around, however, Oliver had opened her door, helped her out, and walked beside her, his hand on her back.

She tried to swallow down the knot that had formed in her throat. How would they people react to her being here and being with Oliver?

The preacher welcomed her warmly, as did his wife. But from the edge of her vision, Marie saw a small group of people her own age looking and snickering. She stiffened.

Oliver must have felt her back tense, and he followed her gaze. "I'm sorry. I'm afraid your popularity will suffer when you marry me."

She felt sorry for him. He didn't deserve to be treated the way he had in school. "We're not in school any longer, and it's time they grew up. Besides, there're more important things than being popular." Now if she could just believe that. She didn't care about popularity as much as losing her friends. But if she lost them, had they really been her friends at all?

Oliver gave her the sweetest smile. Although she wished it could be Derrick leading her into church, she could do much worse than Oliver Hartsell. Most others just had never gotten to know him.

After meeting some people and greeting others she knew, Oliver led her toward the Sunday school room in the basement. She felt the stares, but most spoke cordially, especially the adults they met on the way.

She had barely sat down when she needed to use the restroom. That had been happening more since she'd become pregnant. "Where's the restroom?" she whispered to Oliver. She hoped her face hadn't reddened as much as it felt like it.

Alice, a girl who had graduated with them, must have heard. "I can take you." She stood.

Marie lowered her eyes, so she wouldn't have to look at anyone and followed. Alice led her to the women's restroom and waited for her.

When Marie came out of the stall, Alice stood in front of the door like a sentinel not planning to let anyone pass. "I'm dying to know what you are doing here with Oliver Hartsell. I thought you ran with a different crowd."

Might as well get this over with. Maybe if word got out here, she wouldn't have to answer so many questions at the Fourth of July celebration Tuesday. "Oliver and I are engaged." She held up her hand to show her ring as proof.

Alice squealed loud enough to be heard all over

the church. "I can't believe it. You agreed to marry Oliver?"

Marie stood straighter. "I did. I think we've all ignored what a great guy he is. I'm just glad I discovered it before anyone else did."

"You're serious? This isn't some kind of prank or joke?"

"I am as serious as can be." Marie used the no-nonsense tone she'd heard some of her teachers use over the years.

"I didn't even know you were dating or knew each other."

"I got to know him when we had classes together at school and especially during the biology lab we had together."

"I had heard you were dating Derrick Tucker. I know he took you to his prom in Albemarle."

"I'm not seeing him any longer. It didn't work out."

"Really? He's sure better looking than Oliver. But, hey. I wish you the best. Come on, we'd better get back.

The Sunday school lesson was on loving your neighbor. Marie had never heard love emphasized in church this way. Most of the Sunday school lessons in her church were about walking the straight and narrow.

After class, Oliver led her upstairs to the

sanctuary, and they made their way to the pew where his family members were gathering. She noticed most of the men went outside to talk, and she guessed some to smoke before the service began, but Oliver stayed with her. She appreciated that.

She liked the songs they sang at this church better than the music at hers. It sounded more upbeat.

The preacher spoke on the prodigal son, and although she'd heard sermons on it before, never one like this. Reverend Barbee said nothing we'd ever do would cause God to turn His back on us, and He would always welcome us home. Could that be true? Even after what she'd done. Her family certainly didn't seem to think so, and neither would her church. They were all about never failing and judgment if you did.

Chapter Four: Time Together

Oliver wanted to pick up Marie's hand because she looked like she needed some comfort, but he didn't. It might make people watch them even more, and he knew she felt uncomfortable with all the scrutiny.

He didn't like it, either, but he would tolerate it if it meant being with Marie. Most of the staring seemed directed at her, and he didn't like that, but he got his share, too. He guessed he needed to get used to it with someone like her beside him.

It had never dawned on him that she might be ridiculed because of him when he'd proposed, however. He'd never been part of the in-crowd the way Marie had. In fact, he'd experienced a great deal of bullying. They didn't dare try anything physical because they knew he wouldn't tolerate that. He had defended himself well enough the first time anyone had tried that, and no one had tried again. However, they had hurled plenty of insults and barbs his way.

His dad had always quoted that old saying, "Sticks and stones may break my bones, but words will never harm me." He didn't know if he agreed with that. Words had hurt him plenty of times.

He looked at Marie's hands resting in her lap. He needed her hand in his for reassurance, but he didn't move to make it happen. He sure hoped no one started talking bad about her because of him. He had no idea what he would do if they did.

He closed his eyes and said a quick prayer that God would protect her and guide him. He wanted the best for Marie and the baby. With his financial circumstances, he didn't know how he could manage that, but he would sure do everything in his power to make things right.

Seeing too many people begin to head their way after the services, Oliver hurriedly led Marie to the truck. He waited for her to slip to the middle, and he sat on the outside to guard her until the rest of his family came. Some of the younger people started for the truck, but he glared at them with his brow creased and his mouth drawn into a frown, and they got the message not to approach.

"I'm sorry for everyone staring at you today," he told Marie after he felt certain they would be left alone for now.

"It's not your fault, and it would have been even worse if you'd come to my church.

But it was his fault. Didn't she know that? Or perhaps she was just being her usual kind-hearted self. It would have been bad only if you were there with me."

"It would be much worse without you once everyone realizes that I'm pregnant."

He did pick up her hand then since they were alone in the truck. He needed to feel connected with her. "Thank you."

He would have said more, but his parents came. Oliver would have liked to hold Marie's hand longer, but he got out to let his mother in.

"No, you stay put," his mom said when Marie started to get out, too. "I'll take the window seat this time."

Did Mom also want to protect Marie? Had she noticed the stares and special interest?

When they got home, Marie helped get the meal on the table. Of course, Mom had done most of the cooking before they left, and his sisters helped, too. On one hand, he liked that Marie felt comfortable here and that she wanted to help, but on the other hand, he would have preferred she stay next to him on the sofa.

The others went to change out of their church clothes before they ate, but Oliver decided to leave his on. He wanted to look nice for Marie, and he wanted to remain close to her while he could. He'd have to take her home all too soon.

Dad sat in the living room with him. "So, my son is getting married. Hard to believe." His eyes twinkled, belying the regretful sounding words.

"It's actually hard for me to believe, too. Everything's happened so fast, but I couldn't be happier. I guess all this happiness makes it even harder to believe."

"She seems like a good girl. I can tell she has a good heart."

Had Mother told him about the baby? If so, his father had never mentioned it.

"I just wish I had more money saved up," Oliver spoke his thoughts.

"You'll have to do what your mother and I have always had to do – rely on God. That's not a bad thing. In fact, I think it's a good way to start out married life."

Oliver nodded, and he did agree, but Dad's advice didn't make him feel much better. Trusting God when he felt he should be the one providing for his wife could prove difficult. However, who better to trust? God would surely be more trustworthy than him or any man.

"It's ready." Mom had sent his youngest sister, Annie, to call them to the table.

Oliver hurried out of the room. He wanted to be with Marie, to sit beside her, to see to her comfort.

"What did you think of our church?" Dad asked Marie after he said grace, and everyone had their plates filled.

"It seemed...." She obviously stopped to search for the right word. "Less solemn and judgmental than mine."

Dad raised an eyebrow and started to say

something, but Mom interrupted. "Isn't your uncle the pastor where you go?"

"He is, and Daddy won't consider going anywhere else. In fact, he wasn't very happy that I decided to go with you today."

"I'm sorry to hear that." Mom's face showed real concern. "When you and Oliver are married, which church do you think you'd rather attend?"

Oliver had been considering asking that question himself, but he didn't want to appear too pushy. He appreciated that Mom had asked it instead.

He saw indecision spread across Marie's face. "Of the two, I think I'd prefer yours. With time, people shouldn't stare so much, and I did like the preaching service better. Uncle Leonard's always preaching on our failings and God's judgment. Most of his sermons come from the Old Testament. I've never heard a sermon like the one today." She paused. "Do you really think God forgives us no matter what we do?"

"Of course, he does, honey." Mom's voice softened. "As long as we truly repent, He always forgives. Why, there's not a person who has ever lived who hasn't sinned over and over again. It's what we do about it that counts. Look at David in the Bible. He committed adultery and then murdered the husband to cover it up, but God still called him a man after His own heart. Why? Because David was truly sorry and repented; because David loved God and sought to follow His ways. He failed big time, but he earnestly begged forgiveness, too." Mom gave a little laugh. "I'm sorry. I didn't mean to preach a second sermon today."

"You said that very well, my dear." Dad smiled across the table.

The conversation turned to other things, and Oliver sat back and half-listened to the chatter. Occasionally, someone would ask Marie a question and she would answer. This kept his mind from straying too far afield because, even deep in thought, he stayed attuned to her.

"The girls and I will take care of the cleanup." Mom pushed back from the table after they all had finished eating. "Marie, you and Oliver take a walk. I'm sure you could use a few minutes alone."

Oliver stood, too, eager to do as his mother said. He and Marie needed to talk about when they would get married, and he liked having her all to himself.

Marie got up more slowly. "Are you sure, Mrs. Hartsell? I'm used to washing dishes, and I don't mind helping."

"Thank you, honey, but you go ahead now. And call me Louise."

Marie nodded and followed Oliver outside. He took her hand and headed toward the woods. If they walked along the edge of it, they would have some shade.

Marie waited until they got to the first spot of shade before she spoke. "Why did you tell your mother that the baby was yours?"

The direct, pointed question caught him by surprise. "I didn't say that. From our conversation, she just assumed it, and I didn't correct her."

"Why?" Marie asked again.

"I want this baby to be mine." He glanced her way, but he couldn't read how she felt. "I'm going to raise it as my own, and the fewer people who know differently the better it will be for everyone."

"But isn't lying, even by omission, wrong? I remember Uncle Leonard preaching on that once."

Oliver sucked in a deep breath. "Normally, you're right, but I don't feel like I did wrong in this case. I'm doing it to protect someone else much like Rahab did when she lied to the soldiers of Jericho who came looking for the Hebrew spies. We may tell my folks at some point, but you have enough pressure on you for now. I don't think you need any more worries or concerns."

"Thank you," she whispered almost too low for him to hear.

He led her to a log at the edge of the forest. It overlooked a field, and they could barely see the pond in the distance. "When would you like to get married? Your father wants us to plan it soon, and Mom said whatever we decided would be fine with them. They can work it out to attend at any time."

"I'd rather wait until after the Fourth of July celebration on Tuesday. That way, I can truthfully tell everybody who asks that we haven't set a date yet. Then, it won't seem like we're in such a rush."

"Okay." That made sense he guessed.

"Maybe you can come over to the house Wednesday evening, and we can decide then. Mama will want a say in the planning. And Daddy, too, for that matter. He likes to feel like he's in control."

Oliver had already gotten that impression. Had her father's domineering ways made it easier for her to succumb to Derrick's seduction? Was she hoping to find someone she could please? He mentally shook his head. He didn't want to think about the images these thoughts produced.

"May I pick you up early Tuesday morning? If I don't get to see you tomorrow, I'd like to spend the entire day on the Fourth of July with you."

Her look held all kinds of questions, but she nodded. "What time?"

"I don't guess most things will get going too early, although I'm sure they'll be plenty of people downtown getting ready. I'll come by about eight, and we'll take our time, maybe talk some on the way to town."

She gave a weary grin. "For someone who I've

never heard say more than a few words before, you sure have turned out to like talking."

Did she think he'd been talking too much? "I like talking with you." More than just liking, he needed to talk with her, to be with her, but he didn't add that. "Besides, I thought we needed to talk, not only to make plans, but to get to know each other better before we marry."

"Of course. Forgive me if I sounded critical. I would be even more uncomfortable if you didn't talk."

Did that mean she felt uncomfortable now? He hated all this second-guessing, but he imagined most new relationships had it. He wouldn't know, though, because he'd never had a relationship with a girl before Marie. Any that he'd been willing to date had avoided him as much as possible. Thankfully, his family was a loving one or he would have felt totally rejected.

Marie looked at Oliver, trying to guess what he might be thinking. He had grown quiet after her comment about him talking so much. No doubt, she shouldn't have said it, but she had suddenly grown so tired of it all – tired of her parents' disapproval, tired of trying to fit in with Oliver's family, tired of putting on a good front for other people, tired of the scrutiny at church when people stared because she came with Oliver, and tired of Derrick's absence and silence. Had she been nothing but a disappointment to him, too?

She had hoped Derrick would change his mind about marrying her and being a father to their baby after he'd had some time to think about it. So far, that hadn't happened. Perhaps it would when he found out she planned to marry Oliver. Perhaps that would make him realize how much he wanted her.

Oliver was sweet in his own way, but this new side of him wore her down. He wanted a part of her she couldn't give him. It would be good to have a day apart from seeing him tomorrow.

She had a hard time imaging a future filled like this. In the end, she'd just disappoint Oliver like she had everyone else.

"Are you feeling okay?" Oliver finally asked.

"Just tired. Maybe it would be better if I went home now. I can't seem to get caught up on my sleep?"

She could tell he didn't want her to leave yet, but he nodded. "Of course. You've had a difficult couple of days. In addition, all the changes your body must be going through are probably draining."

"Thanks for being understanding." She stood and would have kissed his cheek if she didn't think he would read more into it than she meant.

They walked back to the house, but she let Oliver go in and tell his parents where they were going. She didn't want to plaster one more fake smile onto her face to say goodbye.

About halfway into the ride, Oliver gave her a quick sideways glance. "Are you sure you want to marry me? I don't want you to feel pressured and do something you don't want."

She did feel pressured, and she didn't really want to marry him, but, given the circumstances, any other choice would be worse. "It is the decision I made. I willingly choose to marry you."

His exhaled breath made a funny little sound. "Sometimes I get the idea that you don't like me much."

"That's not true. I've always liked you, even back in school." She could honestly say that. "I could never see why some of the others gave you a hard time. But I want to be truthful with you. I've always seen you more of friend material than anything else. Seeing you as my fiancé, soon to be husband, will take some getting used to and some time."

His sigh told her he wished for her to feel more for him. "Well, I guess friendship is a good place to start. Husbands and wives should also be best friends."

The whole situation caused tears to pool behind her eyes. She didn't want to hurt Oliver; she didn't want to hurt anyone. But she couldn't turn off her love for Derrick like she turned off the water at the kitchen sink, and she couldn't suddenly turn it on for Oliver.

She looked over at him. She did love him in a way, she supposed, but not romantically. She felt more of a Christian type of respect and a budding friendship. He was a good man, but he didn't make her pulse race or her heart jump to attention.

Marie spent most of Monday helping her mother can green beans and freeze corn, so she didn't get the rest she wanted. At least, the busyness helped keep her mind from dwelling on her situation too much.

She dreaded tomorrow, dreaded spending the day with Oliver with everyone watching. Her friends would come unglued when they found out she and he were getting married. She didn't want to answer all the questions they would have.

Chapter Five: Fourth of July Celebration

Oliver came at exactly eight o'clock Tuesday morning as they had planned. He drank a cup of coffee and ate a cinnamon roll she had baked before they left. She didn't know how he could drink hot coffee on such a warm morning, but she drank a coke with him and ate a piece of dry toast. She rarely ate much before ten o'clock these days.

"Aren't you feeling well?" Oliver's forehead wrinkled in concern.

"I have some morning sickness now, but it hasn't been too bad today."

"You should have told me. We could have made this later."

"It's okay. I would rather walk around before it gets too hot."

"If you're sure." He looked at her carefully. "I'll try to find us some shade somewhere in the middle of the day, so you can take a break and rest."

Once they started, she felt a little like a prisoner being led to the guillotine, but she wanted to get this over with and have the day behind her. Perhaps, Oliver would think her lack of enthusiasm stemmed from her not feeling well.

He glanced over at her. "You look nice, but then, you always do."

She looked down at her pale blue, sleeveless shirtwaist. She had picked the dress for its lightweight which would make it cooler. She would have preferred to wear shorts or capris, but her father wouldn't allow her to wear shorts, and she could only wear any kind of pants around the house.

When they got to town, not many people were out yet, mainly just the people setting up. Marie felt as if she had a reprieve for the time being. They parked in a field not too far from Main Street.

"Have you come to the celebration often?" Oliver asked as he helped her from the truck.

"Yes, since it started again about four years ago, but Daddy doesn't like for me to come. He only allowed me to come with another girl he approved of."

"Well, I'm glad you came with me this year."

Marie couldn't say the same, so she said nothing.

Oliver pulled a yard chair out of the bed of the truck and carried it with them. They found a spot to watch the parade, and he set up the chair for her while he stood behind it. His thoughtfulness never ceased to amaze her. They would get their place and sit and talk until the parade started.

As people began to gather, everyone seemed intent on finding them a place, and Marie didn't see anyone she knew well. Some people stared at Oliver and her sitting together, but no one said anything to them.

When the parade began, Oliver moved even closer, so he could point out things, and they could talk about some of the entries as they passed. There turned out to be a good variety, and it had grown since the first one.

No one came up to them as they watched because, except for some roving street vendors, almost everyone sat or stood where they were to see the parade. However, as soon as it ended, the sidewalks became crowded with moving people.

"Marie!" someone called.

Marie turned to see Mary Jane weaving through the people to get to her. Oliver put his hand on her back. Did he think she needed his support? He might be right.

"I'm surprised to find you two here." She sounded out of breath from her push to get there, but Marie knew what she meant. All her friends would be surprised to see her with Oliver.

She might as well get it over with. Marie held up her left hand, and her diamond ring flashed in the sun.

"Is that an engagement ring?" Mary Jane spoke so loudly people started staring.

Marie nodded but didn't have time to say anything, before Mary Jane let out a shrill squeal. Now, everyone around certainly looked.

"You and Oliver?"

"Yes."

She felt Oliver's hand slip down to her side, and it tightened around her waist. He said nothing, but she felt his solid support beside her.

"When did this happen? Isn't it rather sudden?" Mary Jane's eyebrows rose in speculation.

"It might have happened quickly, but when you know you've met the right one, why wait?" Oliver answered for her, his voice low but steady and filled with resolve.

"Well…er…congratulations, I guess." She looked from Oliver to Marie. "You want to come with me, Marie. I'm going to find the other girls. We'll have a blast."

"No, thanks." Marie didn't have to think twice. She knew she'd be in for heavy interrogation if she went. "Oliver and I have plans."

Mary Jane paused. "Oh? When is the wedding, then?"

"We haven't set the date yet, but I'll see that you're invited."

"You do that." Mary Jane hurried away almost as fast as she came, no doubt in a hurry to spread the news.

A variation of the same scenario played out over and over all through the morning. The only thing Marie got to watch much of was the beauty pageant, and that only happened because most of the girls her age watched it, too – those that hadn't entered the event anyway.

Marie saw Derrick among the audience watching the contestants on the makeshift stage. His eyes were glued to the young women, so he didn't notice her. She tried to keep from watching him because she didn't want Oliver to see where her attention had gone, but her eyes were pulled to him all too often, and her heart started doing some type of jitterbug.

"You're prettier than any of those girls up there," Oliver whispered in her ear as his face flushed with embarrassment.

Did he really mean that? He didn't seem to be the kind of guy to say something he didn't think to be true.

Derrick might have said the same thing, but he would have been so smug and smooth she would have doubted his sincerity. However, she would have still been glad he'd said it. Didn't it only prove how much he cared about her feelings?

"You know the pageant isn't just based on beauty," she told Oliver. "The one who collects the most money for the fire department gets the crown."

"That doesn't change the fact that you're the prettiest girl here. Are you getting hungry?" He changed the subject.

"I am." She suddenly realized that she should have packed them some lunch. The restaurants that were open would be too crowded to get in.

"Let's go to the truck. I had Mom pack us a cooler of food this morning."

"I don't know what's wrong with me. I should have thought to do that."

"It's no problem, and you've had a lot on your mind lately. I think it made Mom happy to help out in some way."

The temperature had to be well over a hundred inside the truck, even though they'd left the windows rolled down about an inch. But Oliver pulled an old, thin quilt from behind the seat, and picked up the cooler he had secured in the back. He led her to a small clump of trees not far from the truck, spread out the quilt in a spot of shade, placed the cooler in the middle, and sat down beside her.

He opened the small cooler and began to unpack it. I think Mom made deviled egg or ham sandwiches. Which would you like? The ham is from the farm and not store bought."

"Oh, I love deviled egg sandwiches." But then on the second thought, he should have his choice, too. "But I like ham, too, so you choose which you'd prefer."

He smiled tenderly. "Then, I choose the ham."

He pulled out two slices of pound cake after the

sandwiches, and then two RC colas. "I stopped by a store on the way in and got the drinks. We don't keep any at the house.

"This is quite the feast." She took a bite of her sandwich, and the flavor burst in her mouth. "This is truly the best deviled egg sandwich I've ever had."

Oliver's grin widened. "I'll tell Mom you said so."

Marie looked away. One would think Oliver saw keeping her happy as his main purpose in life, and it made her uncomfortable. It didn't seem fair that she would never love him as he deserved, could never respond to him in the same way.

"Are you sure you want to marry me, Oliver? I'm not good enough for you."

His smile fell away instantly. "You've got that backwards, now. You ask anybody around." He stretched out his arm and swept it in a semicircle, indicating the crowds in the distance. "I'm the one not good enough for you."

"But that's because they don't know you." She started to put her hand on his arm, but then pulled back. What was she doing? If she didn't stop, she'd give him the wrong impression, and he would begin to think she cared for him.

His smiled returned. Oh, yes. He had misread her words.

"I don't want to give you false hope, Oliver.

I'm not in love with you." She looked away, afraid that she'd been too blunt and cruel. But if he knew now, he could choose to walk away before they married.

She saw his smile had vanished again when she looked back. "I know that you don't love me like that now, but things can change. None of us know what the future holds."

She wanted to tell him that nothing would change. She knew she would never love Oliver, but she'd already said as much, and he refused to accept it. She didn't want to keep belaboring the point, and she didn't want to argue.

"What would you like to do now? Do you want to go to the carnival? He seemed eager to change the subject, too.

"Not yet. It's so hot, and they don't have any shade down there. Besides, I think they close down around two o'clock and don't open up again until five. Did you not want to go to the greased pole event, the horse races, or try to catch the greased pig?"

"Some of those have already been held, but I just wanted to stay with you. They don't really interest me that much unless you want to go."

She paused to listen. "I hear some music coming from the stage area. Want to go check it out?"

"Sure." He began to gather their things.

When they got to the truck Oliver looked around. "I'm going to look for a restroom."

"I'll wait for you in the shade of that building up there on the corner." She had already gone a couple of times that morning but didn't need to right now.

She stood, leaning against the building and watching the people walk by. They all looked happier than she felt.

"Well, hello, gorgeous."

She jerked her head around to see Derrick. Her heart started doing jumping jacks.

"Hello, Derrick." Somehow, she had managed to keep her voice calm and steady.

"Surely, I didn't see you with Farmer Boy, now, did I?"

His tone irritated her. "And what if you did?" She looked around to make sure no one could hear her and dropped her voice to little more than a whisper. "My baby needs a father, and his real father isn't man enough to take the job."

"Whoa, here." He put up both hands. "Where did my sweet Marie go, and why is this battle-ax in her place?"

He glanced behind him as if he knew Oliver would come from that direction. Had he been watching them? "Does he know about the kid?"

"Yes. I wouldn't marry him without him knowing. I wouldn't use him like that."

He looked up over her head as if he didn't want

to face her. "I wish you wouldn't marry him. You know he's not the man for you. I am."

"Is that a proposal?"

He turned red. "You know I'm not ready for a wife and family, but we're good together, darling. I don't want to lose you to a clodhopper like Oliver Hartsell. You don't want him, either. I know you don't."

"My father is a farmer, too."

"Yeah, but he only farms on the side. He also has a good-paying job at the bank. Let's do something together tonight. Where can I pick you up?"

He still wanted her, and that made her feel some better. However, he still refused to marry her, and she needed to make the right choice for her baby.

She saw Oliver come into sight and head toward them. "Goodbye, Derrick." She hurried forward to meet Oliver, not looking behind her. Hopefully, Derrick would fade into the crowd, and Oliver hadn't noticed him.

Oliver felt another grin spread across his face when he saw Marie hurrying toward him. He must have started to look something like Howdy Doody.

He'd had a perpetual smile on his face most of the day, but he couldn't help himself. A whole day spent with Marie would make any man smile.

She might not be in love with him now, but he could tell she liked spending time with him. He had no doubt love would come. Yes, he had plenty to smile about.

They walked around, and people came to Marie in swarms, asking to see her ring or numerous other questions. He knew Marie had always been popular, but he didn't know she had this many friends or even acquaintances.

He tried to stay in the background unless Marie needed him, but he felt everyone's stares. He knew they couldn't believe that Marie had agreed to marry someone like him, a nobody. Or worse, an egghead.

With her usual patience, Marie answered all their questions in some way, although at times she gave a vague reply and changed the subject. She showed her engagement ring again and again and acted proud to be wearing it. Whether intentionally or not, she often held it up so that it caught the light and looked dazzling.

His heart swelled as he watched her. He couldn't blame her friends for not believing she'd agreed to marry him. He could hardly believe it himself.

As her steps grew labored and her face began to

pinch, he knew she needed to rest. "Are you tired?"

She nodded, and he led her toward the truck. "Do you want me to get the chairs or the blanket out?"

"The chairs. I wouldn't feel comfortable laying down out here for everyone to watch, and my back needs something to rest against."

He had hoped the afternoon sun would leave some shade on the east side of the truck, but it remained too narrow to cover them entirely, so they walked to the clump of trees where they'd eaten lunch.

He set up the two folding chairs close to each other, and she sat down and leaned back closing her eyes. Now, he could stare at her all he wanted.

"I think the worst may be over," she said with her eyes still closed. "With as many people as I've talked with, surely everyone knows that we're getting married by now. The ones who don't should be far and few between."

He'd thought she'd fallen asleep, but apparently not. He reached over and took her hand hanging limply on the chair arm. "We can go home if you've had enough."

She opened her eyes. "No, I'd like to stay, go on a couple of rides, and see the fireworks." She paused. "If that's all right with you."

"Whatever you want is fine with me." He wanted to spend as much time with her as he could.

She closed her eyes again as if they'd grown too

tired to hold open. "You're easygoing. I like that about you. So different than my father...." Her voice trailed off and he knew she'd fallen asleep.

The carnival had started when Marie awoke, so Oliver knew it had to be after five. At first, she appeared confused, but then looked at him and smiled. "How long have I been asleep?"

"Not quite two hours."

"Oh." She straightened and rubbed her neck. "I'm sorry. You should have wakened me."

"I thought you needed the rest."

She stretched. "I did, but I haven't been much company."

"You have been very good company. None better." He meant that, too.

"And you're also easy to please." She added to the comment she'd made before she fell asleep.

"I'm glad you're beginning to see some of my good qualities," he teased.

But instead of smiling, she grew serious. "I've always seen your good qualities, Oliver, even back in school. But I don't want you to misconstrue what I'm saying. I don't think I'm ever going to fall in love with you. I think friendship is a much as we can hope for. Are you sure you still want to marry me?"

He swallowed. Why did she keep bringing this up?

As if she'd read his mind, she said, "I don't

want to hurt you, but I want you to know what you're getting into. Can you handle a loveless marriage?"

He didn't want to think about that. She might not believe it now, but she would come to love him, wouldn't she?" She already appreciated how he treated her. He would take that as a good start. "If you can put up being married to a geek whom very few think much of."

"I don't put nearly the emphasis on status and popularity as most of my friends do. There're a lot of things more important than that. Most of the popular crowd are pretty shallow, and I figure I'd lose contact with most of them after graduation, anyway. My real friends will stick with me no matter what, and the others don't really matter that much."

He wanted to take her in his arms and kiss her, but this wasn't the time and certainly not the place. Besides, with her still saying she didn't love him, he needed to be patient and wait. "Are you ready to tackle some of the rides?"

"In just a minute, but I have one question first." Why did you not make valedictorian? I feel sure you messed up that last report card period on purpose. Did you do it so I would have the honor or for some other reason?

He looked away. He hadn't fully realized how perceptive she could be. "I couldn't bring myself to get up in front of all those people and make a speech. I knew you'd be much better at that than me, and you deserved it just as much as I did."

"I don't know about that. You were several points above me in the standing. But I'm going to get you out of some of that shyness, Oliver Hartsell. Just see if I don't."

She already had, but he didn't tell her that. He might have to explain that just being with her gave him more confidence, and she'd know how much he cared. He needed to hold that bit of information close until she came to love him, too. Otherwise, he might scare her away. He'd likely already said more than he should.

They only rode three of the rides at the carnival, but Marie scooted closer as they started to move. And sometimes, especially on the Ferris wheel, she grabbed his arm, closed her eyes, and leaned her face into his shoulder. He loved it.

They danced a little in front of the musicians, along with a crowd of others, but he didn't know how to dance well so they only slow-danced. He loved holding her, however, and she seemed relaxed in his arms.

They went back to the truck and sat in the bed for the fireworks. He took her hand, and they watched the sky burst into brilliant, sparkling colors and shapes. It reminded him of how he felt beside Marie.

"Ready to go home, now?" he asked after the

popping finale.

She nodded. "Thank you for today. Despite all the unwanted questions, I had a good time."

He helped her down. "It's I who should be thanking you for coming with me. I've never had such a good time."

He secured the things in the back and helped her into the cab. He drove home slowly because he didn't want the night to end.

"You are planning to come to the house tomorrow, aren't you? We'll talk to my parents about the wedding plans and at least set the date."

"Sure. I'm not scheduled to work tomorrow. What time do you want me to come?"

"Why don't you come for lunch then, a little before noon, and we can talk after we eat."

"Thank you. I'll do that." And maybe that would mean he could spend the whole afternoon with her.

Chapter Six: Wedding Plans

Despite all the unwanted attention, the day hadn't been as bad as it could have, but Marie felt beyond exhaustion as Oliver walked her to her door. It had been a packed day, although it would have been worse if Oliver hadn't seen that she rested twice, once at lunch and then again before the carnival rides resumed.

He had been a great companion, and she almost wished she had gone to the prom with Oliver at Oakboro instead of going to Derrick's. Then, she wouldn't have gone out with Derrick at all nor given him her heart.

Going to the prom with Oliver would have caused a stir, though, just like today had. Had he even gone to the prom? She didn't remember seeing him there, but she didn't look for him either. She had gone with Tim, the class president, but they both knew it would be a onetime event. She went because he was the best guy who asked. She hadn't started seeing Derrick yet. That came a few days later.

"Thank you again. I had a good time." She moved from Oliver and started to open the front door.

His hand on her arm made her turn back to face him. He started lowering his head, and she almost panicked, afraid that he wanted to kiss her. But his lips touched her cheek instead of her lips, and she relaxed. "Thank you. It was my pleasure."

She couldn't doubt the sincerity of his words. How he'd acted today proved them. He had been joyful and eager to please all day.

She gave him a smile that she hoped didn't look as drawn and tired as she felt and went inside. She needed her bed.

Her parents were already at the breakfast table the next morning when she went downstairs. She could have turned over and gone back to sleep, but she knew that would cause her father to reprimand her.

She noticed her father had dressed in his work clothes. He must be going to work on the farm instead of going to the bank today. She hoped he didn't expect her to help him as he did sometimes.

"What time did you get in last night?" he asked before she got seated.

"Oliver brought me home right after the fireworks ended."

"I still don't want you gallivanting all about and staying out late, even if it is with Oliver. Maybe I need to be sure he knows what time I expect you home."

Marie wanted to protest, but she knew better. "He's coming over for lunch so that we can set a date for the wedding," she said instead.

Her father set his coffee cup back on the table a

little too forcibly. "How many times am I going to have to feed the guy?"

"We have plenty of vegetables from the garden now, Gunther," Mama said quietly, "and I don't want any to go to waste."

Her father ignored the comment but didn't say anything else. Marie sat down and slowly ate some toast, glad that he didn't continue to complain.

Her father got up and left before she had eaten half her toast. She sighed in relief, finished eating, and got up to wash the dishes.

After she'd finished cleaning the kitchen, she didn't see her mother, so she slipped up to her room and lay on the bed in her capris and top. She would rest as long as she could.

She must have napped for about an hour before she woke up and looked at the clock. Nearly ten o'clock. She'd better go down and look to see what she needed to do for lunch. Most likely, she'd need to pick some vegetables from the garden, and she needed to get that done.

Daddy always expected a big meal when he worked on the farm, but she wanted to cook one anyway since Oliver would be here. She dreaded making wedding plans, but maybe a good meal would fortify her. Since she didn't eat much for breakfast, she always felt starved by lunchtime.

Sweat clung to Marie's face as she hurried up the stairs. She wanted to wash her face and change clothes before Oliver arrived. She'd been a messy cook today, and the spots on her clothes proved it. Her father would want her to wear a dress with company coming, anyway.

Oliver knocked on the front screen door at eleven-fifty. They had all the doors and windows open, hoping a breeze would flow through, but any breeze today felt as hot as the rooms.

Marie went to invite him in, and the smile he gave her eased some of her apprehension. She had no doubt Oliver would side with her on the wedding plans.

She pushed those thoughts away until after they ate. She needed to be pleasant to everyone if her father didn't become obstinate to have his way.

The meal went smoothly. Her father didn't seem as harsh with Oliver around. She had always kept her friends from coming over as much as possible, preferring to go to their house if she could. Maybe it would have been better if they had come over. Her father might have been more pleasant with them, too.

She could tell Oliver enjoyed the food, but he didn't say much. He answered any questions her parents asked him, but never initiated any conversation.

"Oliver and I thought we needed to be making

plans for the wedding," Marie said as she got up to wash the dishes. "I knew you would want a say, so perhaps we can do that after I finish the dishes." She looked at her father.

"Yes, we need to. Time's a-wasting."

"I'll help you clean up," Oliver said. "That will make it quicker."

"No, no." Her mama shooed him toward the living room. "You go talk with Gunther. I'll help Marie."

Marie saw Oliver's reluctance to follow her father, and she knew he'd rather wash dishes with her than to talk with the older man, but she didn't say anything. It would be futile, for her mother had made her intentions clear, and her father didn't believe in a man doing housework. She hurried to get the task completed so she could join them.

"She's going to be a handful and will need a strong hand," she heard her father say as she got near the living room. "The Bible says the man's the head of the household, and you need to take that seriously. You hear me, boy?"

Marie saved Oliver from answering when she entered the room, and he gave her a grateful look. Her mother followed and sat beside her husband on the sofa.

Oliver had been left with a chair and Marie took the one closest to him, wishing they had the sofa, and he could hold her hand. She had a feeling she would need all the support she could get before this conversation ended.

"When would be a good time for us to get married?" she began.

"Humph, the sooner the better." Her daddy glared at her. "Tomorrow would be okay. Next week for sure."

"But we'll need more time than that to get out the invitations," Mama protested meekly.

Maybe Marie wouldn't have to do all the protesting. This might not be as hard as she'd imagined.

"Invitations?" Daddy snorted. "She won't need invitations."

"Gunther, if we don't do things close to proper, everyone will be talking about how rushed the wedding was."

Her father paused to consider this. "How long will that take, then. What's the soonest y'all can be ready?"

"Well, since Marie doesn't want a new dress or a big wedding, I'd say two weeks after we get the invitations out."

"And how long will it take to get the invitations out?" His patience, if he had any, had begun to wear away.

Mama swallowed and twisted the end of her

apron string. "It could take as much as two weeks to get the invitations back from the printer."

"Unacceptable! You'll just have to forget the invitations."

"I think the print shop in Albemarle might be able to do them quicker if I want something basic," Marie told them. "They do their own printing instead of ordering them."

"Well, you can check on it," her daddy said. "But if they can't do it in less than a week, you'll just get married without invitations. We can have it announced in our churches and talk to the ones we really think should attend. What else?"

Marie took a deep breath, wishing she could calm her father's impatience. "I would like to have some flowers."

"How much will that cost?"

"I don't know. Probably around a hundred dollars."

"Ridiculous, absolutely ridiculous. Pick you some flowers and you and your mama do the decorating."

"Daddy, flowers are all I'm asking for. Mama wants the invitations."

"Oh, all right." He still didn't look at all happy.

"And we should have a cake," her mother added.

"You can take care of that, can't you, Erma?"

"It needs to be a special tiered cake, but Della will probably do it for little to nothing. She and I have been friends for years."

"Are you going to have a photographer?" Oliver spoke up for the first time.

Now her father glared at Oliver. "I don't see the need."

"I think pictures would be good to have as a remembrance and to show our children someday." Oliver looked at Marie for her reaction, but she didn't have one. "I'll pay for it."

Her father shrugged. "Well, if you want to waste your money like that, go ahead."

"Are you going to contact the preacher?" Marie asked her father.

"I've been thinking about that. I don't think you should have a church wedding, given the circumstances and what you did. You probably shouldn't even be welcomed in the house of the Lord, and I'm sure Leonard will refuse to marry you once he hears that you're pregnant"

Marie sat back stunned. It felt as if he'd slapped her. "Th-then where do you think we should marry?"

"If you don't want the Justice of the Peace, I guess right here will do." He looked around the room. "You could have it inside the house here or outside, either one."

"B-but, Daddy. I've never thought of getting

married anywhere but in church."

Oliver looked at her in concern, as if he wanted to take her hand or kiss her forehead to comfort her. "We can have it at my church. I'm sure it won't be a problem."

Daddy's nod looked more like a jerk of his head. "Go ahead then, if that's what you want. Your church has always been way too liberal, and I'll expect you two to go to church with us after you're married. But I guess your church will be as good as the Justice of the Peace."

"You will go to our church in the future, won't you?" Daddy asked when Oliver gave no response."

"I'll consider and pray about it," Oliver said. "I'll be the head of our household and will need to make the best decision for us."

Marie almost grinned at how Oliver had turned her father's words back on him, but she didn't dare. However, her estimation of Oliver just went up a notch. He might be quiet and shy, but he would stand up for what was right.

"Well, you don't need me for anything else." Her father stood. I'm going upstairs."

Going upstairs meant he would go to the sitting portion of their large bedroom and read the newspaper in the air conditioning. He wouldn't go to the expense of cooling the rest of the house, but he made sure he had a comfortable place to retire to.

Mother took over. "You two get the license, invitations, and flowers. I'll take care of the cake and get some ladies to help me prepare some food for a simple reception after the wedding. And Oliver, you'll need to see about the church and the preacher. We can talk more later if needed."

Oliver turned to Marie. "Would you like to take a ride with me?"

She nodded. She needed to get out of this house for a while. That would be another good thing about marrying soon.

She felt Oliver's tension as soon as she climbed into his truck. He said very little, so she stayed quiet, too. She thought back over the visit. Had she said something to upset him? If she had, she didn't know what it could be. She hoped he didn't turn out to be moody or have bad moods to stretch longer and longer like with her father.

"What's wrong?" She tried to gentle her voice and not sound accusing. "Have I done something?"

He took a deep breath. "I'm sorry. No, of course not. It's just your parents and especially your father. He shouldn't treat you like he does. So, so…."

"Harsh." She could fill that gap with plenty of words. "Cold. Even cruel at times, and certainly uncaring."

"Has it always been like this?"

She nodded and then realized he couldn't see

her since his eyes were straight ahead on the road. "Yes, although it used to be some better. He had some warm moments when I was young, but he changed sometime after I turned twelve or thirteen."

"I'm sorry," he repeated.

"I am, too." She hung her head, memories she didn't care to remember pouring over her.

He reached out and took her hand. "You'll be out of his house soon. We might not have a lot, but I will treat you right, with love and respect."

She flinched. Love? Was he saying he loved her? She looked at his profile but needed to have a better view of his eyes to tell much. Oh, she hoped he didn't truly love her. She didn't want to hurt him, and he might expect more of her if he loved her.

"I'm sorry to bring up a bad subject." He glanced her way.

Good. He must think she had stiffened from talking about her father.

"We should enjoy this time we have together, so let's talk about something better." He seemed to search for another topic. "When can we go see the house we'll be living in? I'd like to get an idea of what all we'll need to do."

She laughed, but it had no humor in it, even to her own ears. "To be honest, I'm not sure it's even livable. It looks pretty dilapidated from the road, and I have no idea what the inside is like. But we could go there now if you'd like. Daddy already gave me a key, although we could probably get in without one."

Oliver's expression lightened, but would it last when he saw the house? At least, it would give them something to do and talk about besides the wedding or themselves, although the house would still be about their future, wouldn't it?

Oh, if only she didn't feel so lost. Or trapped. By his own choice in refusing to marry her, Derrick was lost to her; love was lost to her. After what she had done, even God was lost to her, or at least her parents, Uncle Leonard, and most of the congregation at her church would think so. After hearing Oliver's preacher on Sunday, Marie didn't know what she thought. She just felt so lost.

Chapter Seven: The Shack

Oliver looked over at Marie in the seat beside him. She seemed lost in thought, so he gave her more than just a quick glance. She never looked truly happy anymore, not like she had at school. Had that just been a front? Had her home situation and a harsh father always weighed on her?

He knew her situation made her burden heavy now, but he wanted to help her carry it. His agreeing to marry her should have done that, but it hadn't had the effect he'd hoped. Was there something else bothering her besides Derrick, the baby, and her father?

"Everything will work out." He took her hand in his, wanting more than anything to comfort her, to bring a sparkle back into her eyes and a genuine smile to her lips.

She tried to smile, but it turned out too weak to really be called one. "Do you really think so?"

"I do. Don't let things defeat you and keep you down." He tried to console her, but he doubted any words would do that. "You're not in this alone. You have me, and you have God."

"Thank you." She seemed to force the words out, and yet they came out in little more than a whisper.

After a long pause, she continued. "I don't think

God is very happy with me right now."

He squeezed her hand. "He is if you have asked for His forgiveness. We all do wrong; we all sin. It's what we do afterwards that makes the difference."

"You don't mean to tell me you've sinned?"

Her teasing took him aback, but he chuckled. If she joked, she must be feeling better. "More than most, I'd say. You went to school with me for twelve years; you should know."

Her face clouded. "I'd say you were often sinned against as people picked on you, but I couldn't name a single incident I remember you sinning."

"I could, but the list would be too long, so I'll forego naming them right now. We're getting close to the house, aren't we?"

Marie blinked and looked around. "Yes, it's right up here on the left. The yard is so grown up it's hard to see the house unless you're looking for it."

"There." She pointed at a place the weeds and grass weren't quite as high. "Pull in there. It's what's left of the drive."

The grass and weeds scraped underneath the truck as he pulled in. "Wait here."

"No, I'll come with you." Marie reached for the door handle.

"Please wait until I check things out. There could be snakes."

She stopped in place, leaving the truck door

hanging open and looked at him. "All right."

He shook his head. He hoped her stubborn, obstinate streak didn't grow too wide. He had never seen that side of her before, but perhaps it had helped her survive her father.

He stomped down a path to the porch the best he could. At least, maybe he had sent any close critters scurrying.

Returning to the truck, he helped Marie out and she followed him to the door. They didn't have room on his narrow path to walk side by side.

He took a better look at the porch. The posts and roof would likely have to be replaced, but some of the floorboards were still firm. He could just replace a few bad boards, and it should be fine. The two rock steps leading up would be fine for now, too.

Marie handed him the key, and he unlocked the door. He had to give it a hefty push to get it opened. The bottom might need to be planed.

Inside felt cooler than the outside, but the stale smell of dank, musty air hit him. "Does it have a basement?"

Marie moved her hand from where she had covered her nose. "Just some type of cellar they used for storage, I think. Things like potatoes and such."

It would definitely have to be painted, but he'd expected that. The wiring looked ancient, but he hoped it turned out to be sound. At least it had electricity.

"How long has it been since anyone lived here?"

"I'm not sure." Dismay showed on Marie's face. "I was a young girl, probably six or seven, and they were renters. My great-grandparents who built it had been dead long before I came into the world."

She had told him the place needed work, so why did she look so stunned at its condition? Maybe seeing it made the reality set in.

"It isn't as bad as it could be. I'm sure the roof is going to need replacing, but I can't see any water damage yet, so that's good.

"It's so dirty and grimy." Marie looked around the kitchen. It had no appliances, one end of the few cabinets hung down where it had become unattached, and a couple of doors where hanging or had come off altogether. The floor had a thin linoleum over it, but it had been worn through in places, showing wide boards like the rest of the house.

"The dirt can be cleaned up. I'll fix the cabinets, paint, and put some new floor covering down, and it will be fine."

She looked at him. "There's going to be so much work, how will you get it all done?"

"I'll call in reinforcements to get it cleaned up. My family will help. Then I'll take care of the things we'll have to have done before we can move in. Some of it will have to wait until afterwards, though." He wouldn't have the funds to do everything at once, but he didn't tell her that.

She looked like she was ready to cry. He moved closer to her side and gently pulled her into his arms. "I think it can be a good starter home for us. I'll make it the best I can. I think we can be happy here."

She burst into tears.

"Sh-h-h. Don't cry, honey. Think on the bright side. You'll get to pick out the colors you like, and I bet you can sew some pretty curtains to spruce up the rooms. Why, when you get it decorated, I'm sure the house will be lovely." He rubbed her back.

She finally pulled back, and he wiped away some of her tears with his thumbs. "Shall we have a look at the rest of the house? The kitchen and the bathrooms are usually in the worst shape."

"Bathroom," she said.

"What?" He wasn't sure he had understood her.

"There is just one bathroom, and it isn't much. Someone along the way turned a closet into a bathroom, but there're just a toilet and a sink. There's no room for a tub or shower."

"Well, at least we won't have to run to the outhouse. And as soon as I get the other things taken care of, we'll see about putting in a full bath."

She gave a little laugh at his comment about the outhouse. "I'm glad you can look on the bright side of things." She sounded serious and not sarcastic.

"Hey, things could be worse. "We have a place

to stay when we couldn't afford to rent. And although my parents would try to make room if need be, our house is overcrowded as it is. Believe me, this will be better."

She took a deep breath and straightened her shoulders. "You're right. We'll have a home, and we'll make it cozy."

"That's my girl." He gave her shoulder a squeeze but let his arm drop when he saw her expression. Maybe the house wasn't the only thing bothering her.

"You seem to remember a lot about the house." He changed the subject.

"I didn't, but I asked Mama about it. She knew much more than I did."

The days that followed turned busy. As soon as he got off work, Oliver would go by the house. Often his dad and older brothers would already be working, cleaning and scrubbing, which had to be done before many repairs could be made or any painting done. They had already taken care of the yardwork, and that had made a big difference in the appearance of the place.

As soon as he got there, they would begin replacing boards, nailing up cabinets, and making sure everything was sturdy. His father would help, but he didn't want to do much without Oliver's presence and okay, unless they had already talked about it and planned what to do.

Not long after he got there, Marie would come, bringing their supper. She went over to his house around four and helped his mother cook it. Oliver liked how well the two women got along. Then, Marie would stay and help until he got ready to leave.

During the day, Marie and her mother worked on wedding preparations. He had already contacted the preacher and they had the license. At the end of next week, he would be a married man. Excitement flowed through him. He could hardly wait, although he needed to. He certainly had enough to do.

Work on the house suddenly came to a standstill. Oliver's money ran out, even though his parents had given them a little money for a wedding present.

He hadn't seen Marie alone since they'd first looked at the house together, so he called her. "Would you like to go somewhere tonight after I get off from work?"

"Sure. Where would you like to go?" she asked.

He wished the theater hadn't burned down, but then he didn't want to spend much money right now. "I'm not sure. I guess we could just ride around." But even that would take gas.

I have a gift certificate to Barbee's Grill a friend gave me for my birthday and I've never used," Marie told him. "Would you like to eat there for supper."

Oliver didn't like the idea of her paying for their meal, even if she did have a certificate. "I don't know. Perhaps you should use your gift for yourself."

"There's enough for two to eat, so who do you suggest I take with me?"

Although her comment did sound rather sarcastic, she had a point. "All right, then. If you're sure."

He hadn't meant to talk to Marie about the house, but after they'd ordered, he found his worries pouring out. After all, the wedding would take place in just a few more days.

"We can make do." Marie sounded more confident that things would work out than he'd ever heard her. "I think Mama would let me borrow the hot plate and an ice cooler. It will mean we'll eat more simple meals, but it won't be for long. We can manage."

If they hadn't been in public, he would have kissed her, regardless of the fact that he wanted to wait until the right time when she seemed ready. "I guess we might be able to get the appliances on a payment plan, although I hate the idea of going in debt. It makes me feel constantly behind and trying to play catchup."

She studied him with her head at a slight angle. "You know, this is the first time I haven't seen you looking at the bright side of everything. It makes you seem more human."

"Oh, I'm definitely human, flaws and all." He didn't want to tell her he had been trying hard to make her like him.

He almost laughed. He'd tried to impress her by being positive, and she seemed to appreciate his worries and want to make him feel better. Go figure.

Oliver noticed some of the people staring at them and whispering. He hoped Marie didn't notice.

Their food came, and they grew silent as they ate. He planned to ask Marie what else needed to be done for the wedding when they finished.

A group of girls in the back corner began laughing. As they did, their voices got louder.

"Can you believe she plans to actually marry him?"

"I thought she had started dating Derrick," another voice said. "She went to his prom with him. I would have stuck with him. He's got so much more to offer."

"Well, I wouldn't be seen with either one," a third girl said. "Oliver is a loser, but Derrick's a playboy, and he likes the innocent, naive ones. He has a string of broken hearts behind him."

Marie's well-liked." The first girl spoke again. "She could date just about anyone she wanted to, so I don't understand why she would marry Oliver."

"Who knows." The third girl laughed. "Maybe there's more to Oliver than we would ever guess. Don't they say to watch out for the quiet ones."

"Well, he's so shy who could tell?" Another voice said.

Marie stared down at her plate. Was her chin quivering?

He would have liked to take her hand, but she had them in her lap now. "Ignore the gossips. We knew they would be a problem. They're just spewing venom and showing their true colors."

She looked up at him, her eyes watery. "But those are supposed to be my friends. I know them.

"I'm sorry." He didn't know what else to say. It broke his heart to see her upset, and it was his fault. She wouldn't be the subject of such gossip if she hadn't agreed to marry him.

"Except for you, Oliver, the gossip would be worse in a few weeks." She looked around. "Can we go now?"

How had she managed to know what he'd been thinking? "If you're ready. He had finished eating but she hadn't.

She nodded and stood. He paid and then followed her outside. He would distract her by talking about what they yet needed to do for the wedding on the way home.

The next day, Mr. Little saw Oliver's long face and asked what was wrong. Oliver got a discount on the materials they carried at the hardware store, but Mr. Little didn't carry most of the things he needed. He still needed to paint, put down flooring, and buy appliances. The paint and flooring might wait, but it would be hard to live there without a refrigerator or stove.

"You can take anything you need," his boss said. "I will start you an account, and you can make payments as you get paid. I won't even charge you any interest."

"Thank you." That would help some, although Oliver hated feeling behind or in debt. But paying Mr. Little back wouldn't take as much of his paycheck as he'd been giving his family, so he should be able to manage. And, as Marie had pointed out, he needed to start thinking on the bright side again.

Chapter Eight: The Unexpected Shower

Marie kept hearing her friends' voices playing like a recording in her mind as she sewed curtains for the little house. Her mother had reluctantly parted with some of her precious stash of cloth, but the excitement she had initially felt at making them had dimmed. She'd planned to hang them to surprise Oliver and do her part in making the place livable, but the hurt she felt at what she'd heard yesterday, had taken away any happiness in the project. Even Oliver had been more somber than usual yesterday.

Her friends had actually laughed at her and belittled both Oliver and Derrick. Yet, Oliver had only been concerned about her and not what they'd said about him. He must have grown accustomed to their scorn, but she hadn't. She'd never imagined that they would talk about her so, as if she were stupid or something.

And were they right about Derrick? Was he a playboy who had loved and left a lot of women already? She tried to think of what she knew of him, but he had gone to school in Albemarle, and she didn't know that much about him. However, his grandparents lived in Oakboro, so he'd spent a lot of time here, and almost everyone knew of him.

In the short time she'd dated him, however, he

had treated her so special that she'd fallen in love with him quickly. And she knew he loved her, too. He had changed some after she'd told him about the baby, but they'd both been upset over that.

At the Fourth of July Celebration, he had indicated he still wanted her. She just wished he wanted her enough to marry her. Did that mean he didn't really love her? Oh, she hoped not. But then, it wouldn't make any difference after Saturday, would it? She would become another man's wife then

She wiped the tears from her eyes, so she could see the sewing machine. She needed to get this finished and quit thinking so much. Whatever happened between now and the wedding would be up to Derrick. Surely, he would hear of the wedding and would change his mind and marry her himself. Maybe he would show up Saturday and she could marry him instead of Oliver.

Her heart almost hurt from thinking of marrying Derrick and not Oliver. And strange, she didn't know if the pain came from hurting Oliver or from being afraid Derrick wouldn't come. She didn't want to think what such a rejection might do to Oliver.

And the scandal of it all. She could hardly imagine that herself. But it would be right for her to marry her baby's father, wouldn't it?

It would truly be a shame to leave Oliver at the last minute after he'd worked so hard on the house and trying to make things right for her. But this was her life, her whole future. How could she choose someone she didn't love over someone she did?

As soon as she finished the last stitch on the final curtain, she ironed them. She hated ironing on a hot summer day, but she wanted to get her project finished today.

She borrowed her mother's car and drove to Teeter's to buy curtain rods. She had considered driving nails and hanging them on a string, but she decided to do it right instead of improvising, even though it would take a chunk out of her meager savings.

She wished her father would allow her to get a job, but he never had. He wanted her working at home.

"These look really good." Oliver stood looking over the final room where she'd hung the curtains

Will, Oliver's brother, had helped her put up the curtain rods. He and his father had been working there when she arrived. She had to admit the curtains did brighten up the rooms and went a long way in making the house look homier.

He swung his eyes back to her. "Are you ready?"

What did he mean? Ready for what – the wedding, moving in here, the honeymoon night, married life? It didn't really matter what he meant. She wasn't ready for any of it.

She zeroed in on the easiest to answer. "We have everything ready for the wedding, except the last-minute things, that is."

He looked at her lips but kissed her cheek, putting his arm around her waist right before he did. His father and older brother were working near.

He had been sweet, not pushing her to do things she didn't feel ready for. Would he be like this on their wedding night, too? She could hardly imagine such a thing. Her limited experience with men had shown her they liked physical contact. Derrick sure had.

She mentally shook herself. When would he stop invading her thoughts? Would time truly erase his memory? She doubted it.

Oliver moved to help the men paint the bedroom they would use. She had picked out the paint color, a pale eggshell blue.

At first, she wondered why they were painting that room first. Why not the living room or kitchen, the rooms more people would see. But then she knew. He wanted the bedroom to be nice for their wedding night.

Lord, help me! Was it right to call out to God for such a thing? Would He even listen to a sinner like her, one who had strayed so far from His commandments?

"I'm going," she told Oliver. "I need to get Mama's car back. Daddy's probably going to be mad as it is. He doesn't like me to go anywhere without his permission, especially not in the car."

Concerned lined Oliver's face. "I wish you could call me here if you needed me but call Mom. She'll send someone for me if it's important."

She nodded, but she didn't think her father would hit her this close to the wedding. If he decided to keep her from marrying Oliver, that might be good. But then it wouldn't be good when she started showing her pregnancy. The trap she had put herself in grew tighter all the time.

"Just because you're getting married, don't mean you can go galivanting around at your pleasure, young lady." Daddy's voice hadn't lowered since she'd gotten home. "You are still under my roof and subject to my rules." He'd always talked more like a farmer than a banker.

"She just went to town to get some curtain rods and by the little house to hang them," her mother tried to explain.

"Don't go trying to take up for her, Erma. She had no business leaving the house without my permission. She had no business spending her time sewing curtains, for that matter. There'll be plenty of time for that after she's married. She should be helping you in the house and me around the farm now to pay for her upkeep. Why, no telling how much this wedding business is costing me."

Not much, Marie thought. She hadn't bought a wedding dress and didn't plan to have attendants. She'd only sent out a handful of invitations. Reading one at hers and Oliver's church would suffice for all but family who didn't attend those two churches.

Mama's friend said she would make the cake as her wedding present, and the flowers to decorate the church would be around fifty dollars. The women Mama knew at church would be furnishing most of the food for the reception. Daddy would surely get out for less than two hundred dollars, and likely closer to a hundred.

But she didn't say any of that. Her father's anger raged hot enough already – no use to fan the flames.

Mary Jane had invited Marie over Friday afternoon, and surprisingly, her father had said she could go. Maybe he felt more generous toward her this last day she'd be living with her parents.

"We need to get together to celebrate your last day of freedom," Mary Jane had joked.

Marie had never been free, though. She would be moving from her father's heavy thumb to Oliver's. However, she didn't think Oliver's would be nearly as heavy. Maybe they should be celebrating her move into more freedom.

When she got to Mary Jane's house, cars were everywhere. What was going on? Had something happened?

"Surprise!" a room full of girls shouted as she entered.

Mary Jane smiled. "We thought you needed a shower before you start married life."

Marie looked around stunned. All her friends were here, close ones and those she didn't know as well.

As she noticed the girls who'd been gossiping at the grill, she stiffened. The hypocrites. She wondered how many had come from curiosity or just wanted to gather more fuel for their gossip.

She forced a smile on her face as she saw all the gifts. She and Oliver had almost nothing. Whatever they brought would be needed.

"Were you surprised?" Mary Jane asked as she helped Marie load up the car.

"Completely. Thank you. I can use everything. Did my parents know about the shower?"

"Yes. I wanted help in making sure you came."

So that was the reason her father had agreed. He wouldn't want to appear hard-hearted and uncaring to the good folks of Oakboro.

"This is going to change everything, isn't it? You're the first in our main group to get married. I still can't believe you're marrying Oliver Hartsell." Mary Jane looked at her as if she expected an explanation.

"You know what they say about the quiet ones." Marie tried to sound light-hearted. "I think we've all missed what a treasure he is." A lot of truth resided in those words, she realized.

"Really?" Mary Jane raised an eyebrow as if she questioned that piece of information. "Well, I wish you all the best, although I can't fathom it myself. How could Olive Oil be a treasure?"

Marie flinched at the cruel nickname many had given Oliver. Her stomach tightened with a touch of nausea, and the morning had long passed.

"Thanks, again, Mary Jane." Marie tried to soften her voice, but instead of hugging her friend as she normally would, she got into the car and drove away. She'd had enough of this kind of friendship, if that's what you could call it.

She drove straight to the little house and saw Oliver hadn't left yet. Good. He could help her carry the things inside.

"I hoped I'd get to see you tonight." He beamed as he came up to the car.

"Mary Jane and a bunch of friends gave me a wedding shower. Could you help me carry it in?"

"Of course. Let me get all the heavier stuff? What is all this?"

"Pots and pans, dishes, towel sets, sheets, and lots and lots of things we'll need."

His smile grew wider. "Wonderful. That was good of them."

"Yes, it was." She didn't want to dim his pleasure. In fact, her displeasure seemed to leave in the brightness of his smile.

They unpacked the things and put them in cabinets or in the rooms they would be used. Marie tried to live in the moment and not think of negative comments from the shower or tomorrow's wedding.

"You seem quiet," Oliver finally said. "Are you feeling all right?"

"I've just been a little queasy on and off today, but I'm better now."

"Good." He closed the cabinet door. "Come here." He held out his arms.

With sudden understanding, she realized this is the first time they'd been alone lately. She moved into his arms with dread.

His arms felt good around her, but as he lowered his lips toward hers, she almost jerked away. She closed her eyes, not wanting him to see her panic.

His lips were soft and caressing, instead of being insistent. They asked for her to kiss them back without demanding anything. The kiss wasn't at all disgusting, but neither did it send her passion soaring the way Derrick's did.

"I'm looking forward to tomorrow evening," he whispered as he pulled his mouth back from hers.

She felt a chill run through her, and it definitely didn't come from a drop in temperatures. The room still held the heat of the day.

"I'll see you tomorrow then." She'd take that cue to leave.

His arm slid down to her waist as he turned. "I'll walk you out."

He opened her car door for her and brushed another kiss across her lips. As she drove off, she realized that life would be a whole lot less complicated if she could love Oliver.

Chapter Nine: The Wedding

Oliver awoke early the next morning, surprised that he had slept at all as excited as he'd been. Marie had come by the house last night, and they'd had some time alone for the first time in days. On top of that, he'd finally gotten to really kiss her.

He closed his eyes. It had been so wonderful he could still feel its effects. All sorts of things started happening to his body from just reliving it. Her lips had been warm and sweet and enticing, just as he knew they would be – just as she was.

And this would be his wedding day, the day he got to marry this wonderful woman and make her his wife. He could do without the actual ceremony, but at least she hadn't chosen to have a big, fancy one. Yet, he would have even endured one of those to get to marry Marie.

He jumped out of bed, eager to start the day. The sun began to rise in an array of vibrant colors. His wedding day would be a beautiful day – a beautiful day indeed!

After breakfast, Oliver went by the little house. He wanted to make sure everything would be ready, at least as perfect as he could get it, and he wanted to do some special things in the bedroom. For one thing, he wanted to move in the few second-hand pieces of furniture he'd found and put the sheets on the bed.

He might also be able to find some wildflowers around. He would have asked his sisters to collect some, but he felt too embarrassed to do so. No, better if he did it himself.

He got home in time to eat with the family. His brothers teased him merciless until their parents told them to stop. He hurried to finish and then went to get ready. The wedding would be at three, and he planned to take his time getting ready. He wanted to look the best he could for Marie.

An afternoon had never crept so slowly. Why didn't time move like this when he and Marie were together? It flew by then. But after this, he wouldn't have to leave her as much. Just to go to work and then he'd know he'd get to see her as soon as he got home. He grinned. *Thank you, Lord.*

He went to the church early, but he wanted to make sure he arrived before Marie and any guests. His family would come a little later.

At first, he sat on a pew, bowed his head, and prayed. He prayed he would be the husband and father he should be, that he'd be able to provide for his new family, and that God would direct him. He felt better after that.

He looked around. The sanctuary looked nice with the way the florist had arranged the flowers. He recognized the daisies, but he tried to recall the name of the blue flowers. He knew Marie had told him. Cornflowers if he remembered correctly. The blue and white stood out, along with the yellow centers of the daisies.

When he heard some noise outside, he moved to the room he'd been assigned to wait in. They hadn't had a wedding rehearsal since they weren't having any attendants, but the pastor's wife had given them directions on what to do. He hoped he remembered his, but it shouldn't be that hard.

Just in case, he mentally recited what he should do – walk out when the preacher did, wait for Marie to come down the aisle on her father's arm, say "I do" when the preacher asked him to, put the ring on her finger, and kiss her. It sounded easy enough, and he only had to say two words.

Time was released from its shackles the moment Oliver heard the music begin. Just when he wanted things to slow so he could enjoy and remember it all the more, everything happened in such rapid succession, he could scarce take it in.

After he walked out front with the preacher, he didn't have long to wait until he saw Marie come into view and begin to slowly come toward him. She looked beautiful in an understated way.

She wore little if any makeup, and Oliver remembered her father didn't approve of it. She had pulled her sandy, blonde hair back in a sort of bun so that her pearl earrings stood out, but the style looked more severe on her and didn't do her pretty face justice. She wore a white lacy dress with a tan leather belt that stood out as if to protest appearing at a wedding. Her determined looked softened when her eyes rested on him, and he felt comforted by that.

He still couldn't be sure she wanted to marry him, but he had asked her a number of times, and she'd always said she did. A part of him knew she wouldn't if she hadn't been pregnant, but they got along well, and he felt sure she would soon come to love him.

He shook his thoughts back to the moment and smiled at her, not trying to hide his love. After all, love begat love, did it not?

Marie sucked in a deep breath before she started down the aisle to say her vows to become Oliver's wife. She had looked everywhere, both as she got to the church and as she came around to the front just before the ceremony began. Derrick hadn't come to rescue her.

She smoothed down the lace skirt of her dress. Her father had never liked its see-through lace, but it had an underdress that made it respectable. Maybe that's why she had chosen it from her closet to wear today – that and the fact that it was white, another point that both her parents had protested. They didn't think it was appropriate for a "fallen woman" like her to wear white.

It had a matching white belt that went with it, but she had been wearing it in the last hole, and when she went to fasten it today, it wouldn't meet. Her waist had expanded with the baby.

The dark tan leather belt she wore now didn't really match the dress that well, but she rather liked it. It prevented everything from being too dressy and fussy and made another little statement of rebellion.

She could do this, she kept telling herself as she walked down the aisle with her hand resting lightly on her father's arm. Then, she looked up and saw Oliver.

He looked the most handsome she'd ever seen him in a new taupe suit, white shirt, and gray, blue, and tan tie. His dark hair had been trimmed to lay in perfect order. Her heart beat a little faster of its own accord. She certainly didn't want to admire Oliver, even if he would soon be her husband.

The ceremony went quickly, and Oliver soon held her in his arms and kissed her while the congregation stared. It didn't last as long or contain quite the passion of the kiss last night, so it soon ended, too.

As they turned to walk out, Marie noticed the

people for the first time. Every pew had filled. She guessed people were curious at what they deemed to be the oddly matched couple.

She and Oliver stood at the door greeting people as they left and accepting the many congratulations. Oliver said little but shook everyone's hand with a smile, nodding when they said something.

They went to the fellowship building for the reception, and she saw more wedding gifts filling a table to the side. Good. They could use about anything. She would need to get some thank you cards next week to send out. She had enough money to buy the cards, but she didn't know about the postage. Maybe she could hand-deliver some of them.

She and Oliver cut the cake and had some punch while everyone watched on, but she didn't eat any of the food. As unsettled as she felt, it held no appeal.

The time soon came for Oliver and her to leave. Dread washed over her, and she felt her face heat as they walked out the door hand-in-hand.

She lowered her head as rice peppered them, and suddenly wondered if she would be crawling in the Hartsell's battered truck to drive off. After they'd cleared the crowd, she turned back and tossed her bouquet, an arrangement of blue cornflowers and daisies like those that decorated the sanctuary. Mary Jane caught it and squealed in delight.

Oliver led her to a practically new white Cadillac. She looked at him with a raised eyebrow.

He smiled and opened the door for her. "I borrowed it for the wedding," he answered her unspoken question.

She answered his smile. His efforts and thoughtfulness deserved at least that. Then, as they pulled away with the cans someone had tied to the back rattling, she waved and glued a wide smile across her face because it's what they expected.

"Are you happy with the wedding?" Oliver's voice almost quivered with uncertainty. "I've heard my younger sisters talk, and I know it probably wasn't quite what you'd dreamed of."

"It was fine." She reached over and put her hand on his for reassurance. Given the circumstances, she wouldn't have wanted anything different. But the circumstances were the crux of the whole problem. She tried to lighten her voice. "After all, I chose most of it."

"You looked beautiful." His eyes said the same thing, so she had to believe he meant it. All of a sudden, she was glad she hadn't disappointed him.

"And you have never looked more handsome. Is that a new suit?"

"Yes." He shifted in the seat and looked straight ahead. "I hated to spend the money since we need so much at the house, but I didn't want to embarrass you."

She gripped his hand. "You're not going to embarrass me, Oliver. You always do your best, and no one could ask for anything more.

The truth in those words hit her hard. The problems at school had always been with the hecklers and bullies, not with Oliver. She might struggle with worrying about what others thought at times, but when it came down to making a decision, she would always choose substance over pride.

She hoped she would always choose right, too, but her condition now clearly indicated didn't always happen. Had Derrick been more substance or pride? She didn't want to examine that too closely. She couldn't and still love him as she did, and if she didn't love him, then what she'd done would be really, really wrong.

"Here we are." Oliver pulled into the driveway of their house.

She would be glad when they could afford to paint the outside, but it did have a new roof now, and the yard looked neat.

The house needed so many things, but Oliver and his family had worked hard, and she would look at all they had accomplished instead of what still needed doing. She refused to complain about everything the way her father did.

Oliver rushed around to open her door. He put

his arm around her as he led her toward the house. She tried not to stiffen, even though his eagerness made her want to. When they stood on the porch, Oliver opened the front door, turned, and swept her into his arms.

It stunned her so much she couldn't think. "What are you doing?"

"Carrying you over the threshold." He sat her down inside and proceeded to kiss her.

She did stiffen then. She didn't think she could do what he expected.

"Are you ready to lie down?"

"I-I'm not sure." But she was sure, sure that she didn't want any part of this.

His smile fell from his lips and from his eyes. "Is something wrong?"

She shook her head, trying to prepare the way and soften the words to come. "I'm just tired and a little stressed, I guess."

"We can wait." She could tell he hoped she would say they didn't need to. "I don't want you to do anything you aren't ready for or comfortable with."

"Thank you." She wouldn't tell him that she might never be ready. "I appreciate your understanding."

He kissed her on the cheek. "You go get some rest then. I'll make me a pallet on the floor in the little bedroom."

That's right. They didn't have much furniture

yet. Did she even have a bed in the bigger bedroom?

She went into the room and quickly closed the door, so Oliver couldn't see her expression. Not only did the room have a bed, but there were some other pieces of furniture as well. The bed had been made up and turned down so that it looked inviting. A lovely quilt served as the bedspread.

Two vases of flowers added a sweet perfume. A bud vase set on the small table beside the bed, and a larger one sat on the dresser. Oliver had even placed a rag rug she guessed his mother had made on the floor.

Her eyes filled with tears, and she barely made it to the bed to bury her face into the pillow before the sobs broke forth. She didn't know if she was crying because of her situation or because she had hurt and disappointed such a sweet man, likely some of both.

Marie woke much too early the next morning. She had cried herself to sleep yesterday, but that had happened so early that now she woke up with it still dark.

She lay there, not wanting to get up and face the day. By the time the morning dawned gray and dreary, much like Marie's mood, she had grown restless.

After what seemed like hours, she decided she needed to get up and fix Oliver some breakfast. If she couldn't be a wife to him in other ways, she could at least be a good homemaker.

She sat up and noticed Oliver had slipped her bag of clothes inside the door sometime while she slept. She would need to go back home and pack up the rest of her things to bring over soon, but she didn't know if she would feel up to it today. Oliver had brought his things over already.

She grabbed some pants and a shirt, planning to wash up later. Right now, she just wanted to get out of this dress which had grown terribly uncomfortable.

She found Oliver sitting on the floor in the kitchen with his head bowed and his Bible opened in front of him. She tried to steel her heart, but it ached anyway.

He looked up and gave her a tentative smile. "Good morning. How do you feel?"

"Not my best."

He stood. I'm sorry. Can I do anything to help? Get you anything?"

"No, thanks." She looked around the kitchen, wanting to change the subject. She had forgotten how bare they'd left it. "We never did get a hot plate or a camp stove, did we? I wanted to fix some breakfast."

He looked as if she'd just reprimanded him. "No, I didn't get around to it. I wish we could get the appliances, but my funds have just about run out until I get paid again. I'm hoping I can get some extra jobs soon. Do you want to go out and get something to eat?"

"I really don't feel like getting out."

"I'll go get us something and bring it back here. What would you like?"

"Just an egg biscuit and a cup of coffee with a little cream."

He nodded, started for the door, but then turned back to kiss her on the cheek. "I'll be back as soon as I can. Would you like to go to church today?"

"No, but you go ahead if you want." She couldn't stand the thoughts of everyone staring at them and thinking thoughts that didn't happen.

"I don't want to go without you, so I'll stay here."

She went to the little bathroom and washed up after he left. She guessed they'd have to use a big metal tub for full baths now. That's what her grandparents remembered doing at one time.

It amazed her that Oliver hadn't seemed much different this morning. He might be a little more unsure of himself than he had been, but he didn't seem to hold a grudge against her for not wanting them to sleep together. However, more tension hung in the air between them than before, but that might just be on her side and not his.

Chapter Ten: An Uneventful Honeymoon

Oliver drove to the restaurant deep in thought. He should have expected Marie to feel uncomfortable with the situation, but he hadn't, although he knew she didn't love him yet.

A part of him appreciated that she needed to love a man to sleep with him, but he just wanted her to love him. However, after all that had happened, he knew he shouldn't expect her to be in love with him yet. That would take more time. After all, they had only been together as a couple about three weeks.

He got almost to town when he had another idea. He turned around and headed toward his parents' house. Mom cooked biscuits most mornings, and he would just get their breakfast there. Seeing his family would bring him some comfort and getting a free breakfast would help his dwindling funds.

Thankfully, his father and brothers were out taking care of the chores, so he didn't have to endure their teasing over his honeymoon night, one that he wouldn't let his brothers know never really happened. He found only Mom in the kitchen. The girls must be getting ready for church already.

She came and hugged him the minute she saw him. "And how is my married son this morning?"

"I'm fine. Since we don't have a stove in the

kitchen yet, I came to see if I could get some breakfast to take back. Marie just wants an egg biscuit."

"I just have one biscuit left from our breakfast this morning, but I can make some more if you've got time to wait."

"No, just give Marie the biscuit." He looked over and saw some bacon in a plate. "I'll take an egg and bacon sandwich."

She started putting together his order. "Is everything all right?"

He sat down at the table. What had she noticed? His mother had always been too intuitive when it came to her children.

"I think so." He should have said it was, but he couldn't blatantly lie to her.

She paused. "What's wrong? You know you can talk to me and your father about anything and it will never go any farther."

He found himself telling her the whole story – about the real father of Marie's baby and about last night. He needed his mother's perspective right now, but he hoped she wouldn't think he'd made a huge mistake. Despite last night, he would marry Marie all over again, given the choice. He loved her that much.

"Oh, honey." His mother sat down across from him. "I'm so sorry. You deserve to be loved."

"I feel sure Marie will come to love me in time, but I can't say I'm not disappointed that she hasn't already."

"I'm sure she will." His mother patted his hand. "You are a very lovable person. But it may take more time than you expect for her to get there."

Mother's affirmation meant the world to him. "That's okay, as long as she gets there. I can be patient." After all, he'd waited for her for a long time, never thinking she would actually be his someday.

"Yes, you can," Mother agreed. "You are the most patient one of my children. I'm glad you told me. Now, your father and I can be specifically praying for you."

He nodded in appreciation, feeling the need for all the prayers he could get. He knew when he told her it would be the same as telling his dad, too. They shared everything.

"Oh, by the way, I have an old hot plate here that I bought at a secondhand store several years ago." She stood up. "Shall I get it for you?"

"Yes, that would be good. I'll bring it back as soon as we get a stove. Hopefully, that won't take too long. And I'm going to take that big cooler I bought, too."

Oliver felt better as he drove back to the little house. His mother hadn't been critical and didn't even scold him for not telling her everything earlier. No, she had been supportive as always. And that's exactly how he needed to be with Marie.

"That took longer than I expected," Marie said as Oliver walked into the house with a bag in his hand.

He smiled but looked sheepish. "I decided to go by and get Mom's leftovers. She sent a hotplate and cooler, too."

Marie would have rather no one knew how little they had and how much they would be roughing it for a while, but she held her tongue and reminded herself that his parents weren't as judgmental as hers.

They ate in silence, and Marie felt the tension in her build. She hated that she hadn't pleased her husband, but then Derrick should have been her husband. Although she shouldn't still love him after the way he'd treated her in not marrying her, she did.

Maybe she shouldn't have married Oliver. Now the two of them were destined for a miserable life. If she'd remained single, it would have only been her. But then, she had married mainly for the baby and not herself.

"That tasted good," she told Oliver after they'd finished eating. "Much better than anything from a restaurant."

He looked pleased. Maybe they could find moments of happiness regardless of their situation.

"I'd like to talk to you." He looked so serious that her heart clenched.

Was he going to ask for a divorce this soon? Or rather, an annulment, since the marriage had never been consummated. She looked away as if that could stop him from saying it.

"I understand." Those were not the words she expected to hear.

She looked back at him in confusion. Instead of looking hard and determined, he looked as tender and kind as ever.

"I realize that maybe I expected too much of you too soon. I don't like it, but I do understand that you aren't ready to fully be my wife yet."

She blinked, trying to wrap her mind around what he'd said. "Y-you don't plan to leave me?"

A panic crossed his face. "No! No. I will never leave you, Marie. Whatever gave you that idea?"

"Well..." How could she put all that she felt into words? She couldn't. "I know I've not been very pleasing. You...you must have expected more on your honeymoon night."

He took her hand in his. "That's exactly why I wanted to have this talk. Of course, I would have loved to sleep with you, to hold you close. But you mean much more to me than just that. I want you to be happy, too, and if I need to wait, I will. To be honest, I've loved you for a long time. It may have begun as a crush, but it's grown into much more. I know you don't feel the same way, but I'm hoping and praying you will come to love me soon."

She swallowed down the tears that accompanied the fear. She wanted to tell him that would never happen because her heart would always belong to Derrick, but she didn't. She couldn't dash all his hopes and dreams like that. "I can't make any promises."

He gave her hand a little squeeze. "I know. I'm not asking for any. I will leave it in God's hands and try to be patient." His little grin told her he felt okay with that.

"You're one of the most patient people I know." She might not know much more than that about him, besides the shy student he had been, but she had already learned that much. She also knew him to be tender, thoughtful, and kind.

"I think it might be good to postpone our honeymoon until after the baby comes. That will give you some time without having to worry about what I'm expecting."

She looked down at the floor rather embarrassed by this conversation and at the same time appreciating that she knew where they stood without having to keep guessing. "All right. Thank you."

"I'm going out to explore that shed out back

and see what's in there. I looked in from the door earlier but couldn't tell much. The building seems sturdy, and I plan to bring my woodworking tools over I inherited from a great uncle. I enjoy carpentry, and I hope to get started on some furniture for us." He looked as if he hoped Marie would go, too, but she wanted some time by herself to think.

When he left, Marie sat without moving, trying to process what had happened. He'd told her he would give her time, at least until after the baby came. That would be months. She couldn't believe any man would be that generous.

If he hadn't told her he loved her, she would have thought he didn't find her attractive and didn't care about sleeping with her. But she knew better. She had seen it in his eyes when he looked at her.

She didn't want him to love her because she didn't want him to get hurt when he realized she would never love him back. Yet, a tiny part of her warmed by his admission. It felt good to be wanted by someone.

The morning passed more quickly than Marie expected, although she wished she had all her things. Oliver had a handful of novels among his things, and she took one to read, but she hadn't gotten far in it until they went over to his parents for lunch.

"Can you wear what you wore yesterday?" She could tell Oliver hated to ask her after she'd slept in the dress. "Mom wants to take some pictures. She forgot to take her camera to the church yesterday."

Marie started to say she could just buy some of the pictures the photographer had taken but then realized they might not be able to afford them. She dutifully changed back into the lace dress.

No one at the Hartsell's mentioned them not attending church, and Marie hoped they assumed she and Oliver had gone to her church. She didn't want them to think she might lead Oliver astray.

Mrs. Hartsell acted especially nice and caring to Marie, but she still felt uncomfortable, as if she were mistreating her son by their sleeping arrangement. Guilt wanted to gnaw at her, but she didn't know what to do about it. She wanted intimacy even less.

After the last dish had been washed and put away, Mrs. Hartsell took them outside to pose for pictures. Marie tried to smile and look happy as Oliver looped his arm around her shoulders, but she felt anything but happy on the inside. He hadn't worn his suit jacket or tie, but if Mrs. Hartsell didn't say anything about it, she wouldn't either.

When they left, Mrs. Hartsell sent enough food with them for their suppers, along with some bread and homemade jelly for in the morning. Tomorrow, Marie would ask Oliver to take her to her old home to get her things. He had taken two days off from work and wouldn't go back until Wednesday.

"I'm going to the hardware," Oliver said Monday morning after they'd eaten some bread and jelly and drank some water for breakfast. "I think I remember some wooden crates in the back that we might use for a temporary table. Would you like to come, too? We won't be gone long"

Marie shook her head. "I'll just stay here." She still wasn't ready to go out so soon after their supposed wedding night if she didn't need to. "But after you get back, maybe we can go to my parents' and get the rest of my things."

"Sure." He kissed her on the cheek before he left. She liked the gesture, but it continued to surprise her. Her father and mother had never shown such affection.

True to his word, Oliver came back shortly. He unloaded a large wooden crate that had solid ends, slats on three sides, and the top open. He flipped it over in the middle of the kitchen, so the open part rested on the floor.

He went back to the truck, carried in a piece of plywood that extended over the crate about a foot on each side, and nailed it in place. "There, that should work for a little while, don't you think?"

"Yes. I can cover it with a sheet or tablecloth, and it will look nice."

"The hardware didn't have any small wooden crates, but I stopped by the fruit stand and they let me have two apple crates. We can upend them and that will give us someplace to sit around the table."

He brought the two apple crates in and stood them at the table. "I'm sorry we can't start housekeeping with everything you need. I promise I'll work hard to get us what we need."

"This is fine." She didn't want him to feel bad. "It's kind of fun to improvise and make do."

"You're sweet to say so. On a brighter note, there's some wood stored in the shed out back, and my uncle bequeathed me his carpentry tools before he died, so I can begin making us some furniture. It's something I enjoy doing. But come on, we'll go to your parents' home to get your things before lunchtime."

When they drove up her driveway, Marie's stomach knotted. Despite what they lacked at the little house, she realized she'd rather stay there than here. For the first time in her life, she had another home, one not filled with so much criticism and judgment.

Her stomach untightened some when she saw that her father's truck was gone. They needed to hurry before he came back for lunch.

"Come on in." Her mother looked from Oliver to her, and Marie wondered what she was looking for. But she beamed with happiness to see them, which came as a surprise.

"I just came to get the rest of my things."

Her mother nodded and stepped back for them to proceed. Marie led Oliver up to her room. He could carry the things out as she packed. She had left some cardboard boxes in the corner for just that purpose. She'd planned to get more packed before she left, but time had quickly slipped away, and she had done little.

"This is a nice room." Oliver's eyes swept over the bedroom.

"It became my retreat."

She wondered if he compared it to the meager furnishings in the little house. Most of the furnishings came from my grandparents' house when they died. Grandmother even made me the quilts." She nodded to the two folded quilts on top of a trunk at the foot of the bed. "I'm taking those with me."

He picked them up. "I'll just take these down and put them in the cab of the truck."

"Honey." Mama walked into the room as soon as Oliver left. "There're some things stored in the attic, a few pieces of furniture and such. Go up there before you leave and see if there's anything you can use. Your father went to the stock sale this morning, and he won't be back for a while. He won't know they're missing. Why, I doubt he even remembers what's up there. Get anything you want."

"Thanks, Mama." Marie could tell her mother

wanted to do something to help them, and it touched her.

Marie hurried with the packing and then led Oliver to the attic. There were two nice upholstered chairs; a single bed frame and mattress; and a couple of small, occasional tables.

She found some boxes with towels and linens and some lamps she wanted. An old, pedal sewing machine seemed to work, and she and Oliver carried that down, too. There were some mismatched dishes, a box of large fabric scraps, and some other odds and ends that she also took.

When they left, they had the truck filled. She sure hoped they didn't meet her father on the way out.

Chapter Eleven: Unexpected Visitor

Tuesday, Marie spent the day sorting through what they'd brought home yesterday and putting up what she could, along with the rest of their wedding gifts. Oliver offered to help, but she knew he wanted to spend time in the shed setting up his workshop, so she shooed him out.

She had enough room to store the kitchen items in the cabinets there, but without a linen closet or cabinet, she had to leave some items in the boxes. And Oliver definitely needed some things in his bedroom. At least, he had the single bed now and a small table beside it. She didn't like the idea of him sleeping on the floor.

They went to get a few groceries to fix sandwiches for lunch and some ice for the cooler. Oliver said as soon as he got his next paycheck, he would buy a used refrigerator. They could use the hotplate to cook on for a while, but keeping ice in the cooler would be a pain.

When they finished shopping and started to put the groceries in the truck, Kenneth Eudy came out of the Red and White pushing a cart. They hadn't needed to push the cart out for their two bags.

"I want to give you a few more things courtesy of me," he said. "Consider it a wedding gift and a housewarming gift."

Marie stood stunned while Oliver took the groceries Mr. Eudy handed them. He had four bags.

"This is awfully kind of you, and we appreciate it." At least Oliver hadn't lost his wits.

"Yes, she finally said. "I never expected such a thing, but it is very generous. Thank you."

He might not have meant it as such, but it was a good business practice, too. She would definitely buy her groceries from the Red and White from now on.

Marie saw Oliver off to work the next morning with mixed feelings. She didn't mind having more time to herself without thinking about pleasing someone else, but at the same time, she would miss his gentle presence. She'd never met an easier-going person to live with.

About ten o'clock, someone knocked on the door. Marie left the baby clothes she'd been cutting from some soft flannel fabric scraps from the box she'd brought from the attic yesterday on the makeshift kitchen table and went to answer the door. Perhaps it was Mrs. Hartsell. She doubted that it would be her mother or father.

She opened the door and froze. Derrick stood confidently there with a big grin covering his face. "Surprised? Aren't you going to invite me in?"

She took a step back, so he'd have a clear entrance. She would let him in, not because she wanted him there, but because she didn't want anyone to see him standing on the front porch.

She led him to one of the two chairs Oliver had placed in the living room with a small table between them. She sat in the other one.

He looked around. "I can't believe you're living in this sparse place, but then I don't guess Oliver can afford much more, huh? I hear he's always been a loser. What did some people call him in school? Olive Oil, wasn't it?

"Yeah, the jerks." She gave her eyes free rein to pierce him.

"Why did you marry him, Marie? You know we had something good."

"You know why." She had to fight to keep from yelling at him. "You wouldn't marry me."

"All you had to do is have an abortion. Women do it all the time, thousands of them. I did want to marry you but not right now. My parents are insisting that I go to college. You could have had the abortion, we would have become engaged, and as soon as I finished college, we could have married. It might not be too late for that. We could check with an abortion doctor, and divorces happen all the time, too."

"I will not kill our baby, and that's final. Besides, abortions are illegal."

"Yeah, well it's been done for years. I can make all the arrangements. He gave her that puppy-dog look that usually made her give in to him. "What are we to do now then? I don't want to lose you. I feel as if my heart has been ripped out. You can't tell me Oliver makes you as happy as I do. There's got to be something we can do to be together."

She felt her anger slipping. When he talked to her like this, she could believe that anything could happen. Didn't true love often win out in the end?

She shook her head. She needed to make the right choice, no matter how her heart cried out differently. "It's too late. Oliver and I are married, and I won't leave him like this. He's a good man."

Derrick smirked. "But not as good for you as I am. We were meant to be together, and you know it."

She looked away, so she wouldn't see his soft eyes pleading with her. "I made my vow, and I need to see this through."

He huffed and stood. "Well, if you change your mind, you know where you can find me. You can even call…." He looked around and didn't see a telephone. "Or write."

She didn't answer but walked behind him to the door. He turned. "How about a goodbye kiss?"

She shook her head. If he kissed her, she didn't know if she could resist him.

"Later, then." He walked out.

Marie stood staring at the closed door. What did he mean by that? Did it mean that he didn't intend to give up? She started back to the chair but then wobbled to her bedroom instead. She needed a pillow to cry into. She felt so mixed up and confused, crying seemed the only release.

By the time Oliver came home, Marie had had her cry, freshened up, finished cutting out two little sleepers, and was sitting in front of the sewing machine making even seams.

She stopped when she heard him and met him headed her way. "How was your day?"

"Not bad, but tomorrow I'm supposed to help some men roof a house. I hate doing that in this heat, but I'll be glad for the extra money. It's a hot, dirty job, though."

"I'm sorry. Is there anything I can do to help?" She didn't know why she asked the question when she knew she couldn't."

"Just having you here like this when I get home is enough. I've looked forward to coming home to see you all day."

"I've looked forward to seeing you, too." Although true enough, maybe she shouldn't have said anything. She didn't want to give him false hopes.

The radiance of his smile dispelled any misgivings she had. He was an easy man to make happy.

The thought to tell him about Derrick's visit skittered across her mind, but she ignored it. She knew he'd be displeased, and she didn't think he'd let her general information go without a lot of questions about what she and Derrick had talked about. She didn't want to tell him what Derrick had said, and she could think of no honest answers to his questions that wouldn't be uncomfortable.

"Did I hear the sewing machine going? Is it working okay for you?"

"Yes." She didn't mind talking about sewing, something she loved to do. "It took just a little while for me to get used to the pedal, but it works fine. I'm making some baby clothes. Want to see?"

He followed her without hesitation, interested in anything she did, and he really looked at the pale yellow and green pieces she had laid out across the bed. "I'm sure these will be cute when you get them completed. Those curtains you made sure are nice and brighten up the place. They make it feel more like a home."

Her heart swelled at his praise. She smiled her thanks.

"By the way, I brought a big galvanized washtub home. We can use it for bathing, washing clothes, or whatever. I hung it on the far side of the shed, but I might move it to under the overhang of the roof to catch rainwater. What do you think?"

"Just leave it there for now. I'll get it down tomorrow and bring it inside to take a bath, and I don't feel comfortable doing that out back, even if no one can see from the road."

She felt thankful when she went to bed that Oliver hadn't asked anything about Derrick or a visitor. She'd been half afraid that someone might have seen Derrick coming or going or his car parked out front and told Oliver. Yet, she dared not thank God for success at being deceitful.

She hoped Derrick would stay away and not try to contact her again. She didn't like keeping secrets, especially from Oliver. Yet, a tiny part of her, a part she wished she didn't have, wanted to see Derrick again, to hear him say how much he wanted her.

Bringing the tub into the house and warming enough water to fill it turned out to be more of a chore than Marie expected the next afternoon. Oliver had chosen an oblong one, which would make it somewhat easier to take a bath.

It would have been easier to take her bath in the kitchen, closer to the sink, but she set the tub in the corner of her bedroom instead. She didn't want Oliver to unexpectedly come by for something and find her taking a bath in the kitchen.

When she'd finished, emptying the tub turned

out to be an even bigger job. She couldn't lift the heavy tub filled with water, so she had to take a bucket and dip most of it out. To keep from leaving a wet trail of water, she tried to wipe each bucket off with a towel before carrying it out. When she got enough water out, she scooted the tub to the back and emptied the rest.

Then, she brought the tub back into the house, set it in Oliver's bedroom, and began the process of filling it again. He'd said that he'd be roofing today, and she figured he could use a good bath when he got home.

Was it guilt causing her to want to be extra nice to him? She didn't know, but he had been good to her, and she didn't want him to regret marrying her, even if she couldn't be the wife he deserved in other ways.

At times, her resentment wanted to take over, but she didn't resent Oliver as much as she did the marriage and the situation. No, none of this could be blamed on Oliver. He had done nothing but try to help her.

Truth be told, she resented Derrick more than she did Oliver, regardless of how much she loved him. Since he had gotten her pregnant, he should have lived up to his responsibility and married her. So, what if he planned to attend college? His family had plenty of money, and he didn't have to work to support them. Plenty of people went to college when they were married.

She could tell he just didn't want anything to do with the baby, and she didn't understand that. If he loved her like he said he did, why wouldn't he love their baby, too? Why wouldn't he want to be a part of its life? And even worse, why would he want to get rid of it permanently?

She shook her head. Such gloomy thoughts made her feel terrible and didn't bring any answers. She couldn't do a thing about the situation she found herself in. She was locked into circumstances just as confining as before. Well, maybe not quite. Living with Oliver was much easier than living with her father.

When she heard Oliver's truck pull up, she hurried to carry the last bucket of hot water to the tub. She didn't want the water to be too warm on this hot day, but she did want it warm enough to be comfortable.

She looked at the things she'd laid out on the bed for him – towel, washcloth, soap, and shampoo. If he needed anything else, he could get it.

"What's this?" He looked dirty, hot, and tired.

"I took a bath earlier and thought you might enjoy one, too."

His face lit up. "How thoughtful of you. I sure can."

"I'll just go see to supper." She felt embarrassment creep over her, and she hurried to leave his bedroom as he started unbuttoning his shirt.

Oliver leaned back in the tub and let the warm water ease his tired muscles, enjoying the unexpected pleasure. Marie staying to scrub his back would have made it even better, but he couldn't complain. She had gone out of her way to make him more comfortable, and he'd take any progress he could get. It warmed his heart as much as the soothing water warmed his aching muscles.

He moved in the tub, trying not to slosh water over the sides. He likely displaced more water than Marie expected, he barely fit in it, despite having his legs bent to his chest.

After a few minutes of soaking, he washed and got out, wanting to be nearer to Marie. Would he get by with kissing her for her thoughtfulness? He hadn't done more than kiss her cheek since the wedding. But if he kissed her when she didn't want him to, she might stop doing extra things like this for him.

Why did their situation have to be so complicated? He could normally read people pretty well, but he couldn't tell what Marie thought. His gut told him she still didn't want romantic attention from him, but he found it hard to wait, and living in the same house didn't make it any easier.

"Be patient," he reminded himself. "You've only been married four days, and you promised to wait until after the baby came.

"But she could negate that promise if she chose to," another voice said. How he wished that would happen, but he needed to be realistic. No, he needed to give her time and not undo the progress they'd made.

She treated him like a good friend, maybe her best friend, and although he wanted to be so much more to her, he believed more would come in time. She was his wife, living in his home, and that would have to be enough for now.

Oliver woke up wondering what he'd heard. He looked at the clock as the sound came again. Nearly five o'clock. It would soon be time to get up anyway.

He got up and quickly put on his clothes but didn't take time to put on his shoes and socks. It sounded as if Marie had gone to the bathroom to throw up.

He found her on the bathroom floor with her head bent over the toilet. Her retching pinched his heart. He kneed down beside her to hold her head.

"Do you need to go to the doctor today or the emergency room now?" He asked when her vomiting subsided for a moment.

"I think it's just morning sickness, but it has never hit me like this before. It's been mild and wore off quickly." Her voice sounded weak and lifeless.

He dampened a washcloth and wiped her face but lay it aside to help her again when another wave of nausea hit. He wished he could do more.

"Could you help me to bed?" she finally asked in her faint voice. "I think the worst is over for now, and I'm as limp as a worn dishrag."

He helped her stand, but when he saw how she wobbled, he lifted her and carried her to her bed. "Do you need anything? Dry toast, crackers, something to drink?

"Not yet. I'll take something in a little while if I don't have to throw up again." She paused then opened her eyes and looked at him. "How do you know so much about helping pregnant women?"

"Remember, I'm the oldest child in a large family. I've seen Mom experience some of this."

"Thank you. I appreciate your help."

"Always, sweetheart." He leaned over and kissed her forehead.

He sat on the bottom corner of her bed and watched in case she needed his help in getting to the bathroom again. When she appeared to be sleeping, he got a bucket and set it close to her bed.

He'd fix him something to eat and some coffee

while listening for any movement from her. They'd found an old-fashioned percolator in one of the boxes Marie had brought from her parents' house, and they'd bought some ground coffee.

When he could, he needed to get word to Mr. Little that he wouldn't be in today. His sick wife needed him.

Marie didn't wake up until nearly seven. "I feel some better," she told him. "I think I might try to eat some dry toast and drink a little Sprite.

He got them for her. "If you feel well enough, I'll run down to the hardware and let them know I won't be in today."

"Don't do that. I'll be fine. The sickness will wear off soon."

"But what if it doesn't? We don't even have a phone for you to call. No, I'd feel better staying here with you."

"And that would make me feel worse. Think," she pleaded. "This is likely to continue, although I hope it won't be this bad again. You can't stay out of work with me every morning. "I'll be fine."

"Maybe I should start just working after lunch."

She shook her head. "You know we need the money. It's best you go on to work. I'm already feeling much better. I'll be fine, but if it would make you feel better, come home for lunch today instead of packing it."

He looked at her carefully. Some of her color had returned, and she did sound stronger. "Are you sure?"

"Positive. Now, hurry around or you'll be late."

He sighed in defeat. "Well, at least I'm half-ready thanks to my thoughtful wife who provided a thorough bath and clean clothes last night."

She closed her eyes again, but he could tell the comment pleased her. He just hoped she felt as well as she wanted him to believe. He'd come home a little early for lunch to make sure.

Chapter Twelve: An Unexpected Disagreement

Oliver's parents expected Marie and him to eat Sunday dinner with them after church each week, so they drove there after church Sunday. Marie didn't appear to mind and seemed to look forward to it. He was just glad that her morning sickness had never been debilitating again, and it seemed to be subsiding. Otherwise, she wouldn't have been able to go to church or to his family's dinner.

His family didn't always have a lot of different dishes at a meal, and, depending on what meats his dad had been able to butcher and what Mom had left in the freezer from hunting season, they didn't always have meat. However, during the summer months, they always had vegetables from the garden.

The family needed another freezer with so many mouths to feed, but they couldn't afford one. However, they did seem to be doing better than in some years. Oliver could remember times he didn't get all he wanted to eat because they just didn't have it, but none of them starved. They always managed something.

He'd bought an affordable, used refrigerator for the little house when he got paid. The added appliance made it easier for Marie to fix their meals, although she still had to cook on the two-burner hotplate. He hoped to get a stove before too much longer.

"Would you like to go fishing?" he asked Marie when they'd finished cleaning up after the meal. She and he had washed the dishes to give his mother a break. He had rather wash dishes with her than sit in the living room.

She dried her hands. "That might be fun. Today hasn't turned as hot as the last ones have been."

"I'll just go home and get the fishing gear out of the shed and hurry back."

"I'll ride with you. I'll need to change out of my church clothes, and that way you can head straight to the pond afterwards."

"That's a good idea." It made him happy that she liked being with him, too."

Going back to church hasn't been as difficult as I feared," she said as he drove. "Although I've begun to show some, people didn't treat me as a fallen woman. I guess getting married made all the difference."

He winced. He hoped that wasn't the only reason she'd married him. "You're not showing much. Most people probably haven't even noticed yet, but I can't think of anyone in our church that would mistreat you when they do notice."

He quickly dug some worms from the north

side of the shed, gathered the fishing supplies, and got some water to put in the back of the truck while Marie changed clothes. She came out wearing some short pants and a sleeveless top.

She looked down at herself. "I need to make me some shorts. Daddy wouldn't let me wear them, so I don't have any, but they'd be cooler."

He didn't reply because he didn't know what to say. He'd prefer she not wear shorts out in public where men would be looking at her pretty legs, but he didn't want to be controlling like her father. However, it would be fine for her to wear them when it would be just the two of them, like now.

When they got set up at the pond, Marie picked up one of the old but still serviceable rods and reels. "Give me a refresher lesson on how to do this."

He liked being so close to her as he showed her what to do. She cast fine on her first try, but when they went to put worms on their hooks, she looked squeamish.

"Need some help?" He hoped he kept his amusement hidden.

"I guess I do. I don't know what's come over me. Things like this don't usually bother me, and I baited my own hook the first time I went fishing."

"I don't mind." And he didn't. He liked it when she relied on him. With their situation, he felt as if they were courting more than anything else. At least, he wanted to woo her. He smiled at the old-fashioned term.

In the middle of the day, the fish weren't biting a lot, but he enjoyed sitting and talking to Marie. It made for a pleasant afternoon, and apparently, Marie enjoyed being outside as much as he did.

They were still sitting and talking when Marie got her first bite. It surprised her so much she jerked her line and caught the fish. She seemed like a young girl in her excitement as she reeled it in.

He took it off her hook without asking. With the two he'd caught, they'd have enough for supper.

"That was fun," she said as they put their things in the truck to go back."

"Yes, it was. We'll have to try it again sometime. And maybe we could go to Morrow Mountain for a picnic sometime."

"I'd like that." Her face beamed with pleasure, and he sure did like making her happy.

"I'll clean the fish if you want to fix them for supper," he told her when they got home.

She nodded. "I'll pan fry the fish, boil some potatoes, and make some slaw. Do you also want me to fry some cornbread, sort of like pancakes, since we don't have an oven?"

"No, that's okay." He knew it would make it harder on her since the hotplate only had the two burners. "I don't need bread at every meal, especially since we're having potatoes."

"Maybe we should think about getting a large toaster oven if it's going to be a while before we can get a stove."

"We can, but I hope to be able to get us a cooking stove before much longer." He couldn't help but feel guilty that he couldn't provide all they needed.

They settled into a comfortable routine over the next few weeks, and Oliver thought they were growing close. He'd been watching for a good opportunity to kiss her. He just didn't want to do anything too soon and cause their relationship to regress.

"Now that the morning sickness has left," she said as they washed the dishes one evening, "I think I should look for a job."

He nearly dropped the dish he'd been drying. "What kind of job?"

"I don't know. One in Oakboro so I could ride with you." She paused to think. "Maybe at a store or restaurant."

"I don't think that's a good idea, Marie. Your body is going through a lot of changes, and it will be tiring as you get closer to your time."

She huffed. "Pregnant women work all the time, and we can use the money. With me working, we'll be able to furnish the house more quickly."

"We're doing all right, and it won't take me long to get what we need. I think I can get more jobs on the side as the weather cools and people begin preparing for winter. I'm usually the busiest in the spring and fall."

"But if I work, you can't deny that we could do more with the house faster."

"This is the first time I've heard you complain. Please let me take care of you."

"You are taking care of me." She dried her hands on her apron and stepped closer, putting a hand on his arm. "You do a good job of that but let me help. We are partners, aren't we? Let me do my part."

With her beautiful blue eyes looking into his and her gentle touch on his arm, he couldn't deny her. "I don't think it best, but if it's what you want, I won't try to stop you."

"Thank you." She showed her delight by standing on her tiptoes and kissing his cheek. "Mary Jane is supposed to come by sometime this week. I may get her to take me around to some places."

Oliver bit his tongue to keep from saying anything more.

"I got a job today." Marie met him at the door as he got home from work on Thursday. "Mary Jane came by this morning, and I only had to go to three places before I was hired. I start Monday morning and work the breakfast and lunch shifts."

"Where is it?"

"At the Friendly Grill."

"As a waitress or cook?" He said a quick prayer that she would be in the kitchen cooking."

"As a waitress. Isn't it great? This way, I'll be able to make tips."

He walked into the kitchen and set his things on the table to try to calm himself before speaking. She followed him, her features changing to confusion as she judged his reaction.

"What's wrong?" She spoke first.

"I don't think you want to work as a waitress. You'll be on your feet all day, and it'll be hard on you."

"I'm not as weak and useless as you seem to think. I'm healthy enough. I'll do fine."

"You won't want to continue working after the baby comes, so I don't think you should try to start now." He groped for any reason he could think of to discourage her.

"I might. It depends. Your mother already said she would tend the baby for me as much as I needed."

He decided to use his last argument, the one he hadn't wanted to voice. I don't think you want to contend with the rude, flirting men and all the gossips. A lot of men congregate at the Friendly Grill."

She put her hands on her hips. "You're

beginning to sound just like my father."

She couldn't have made a much worse comparison because he knew what she thought of her father's overbearing ways. "I just don't want you to find yourself in a bad situation."

"What bad situation?"

"Being degraded or even groped."

She snorted. "You're jealous, and you don't trust me."

"That's not true, but I know how rough and crude some of these men can be. Some of them think all waitresses are loose women and fair game."

"You're being ridiculous. That might have been true a hundred years ago, but not now. I've already taken the job, and I'm going to work on Monday, even if I have to get out and walk there."

He pushed down his anger and tried a gentler approach. "Just think about what I've said. I know you're worried about all the gossip concerning us. This will only add to it. In addition, you really might get too much unwanted attention from uncouth men."

He put up his hands when she started to argue again. "Just think it over when you calm down. I'll take you to work Monday if that's what you decide, but I really don't think it's for the best."

Marie served Oliver his supper but didn't say a word, and he had sense enough not to try to make her talk. She fumed. How dare he try to tell her what to do! He might be her husband in name, but he had no right bossing her around. It did remind her much too clearly of her father.

And she never expected this of Oliver. He had always been so reasonable and easy to get along with. Perhaps she should have remained single. At least, she would have been her own boss then.

She went to bed not long after cleaning up the kitchen. She could stew in there as well as she could anywhere else, and she didn't have to endure Oliver's disapproving presence.

By Sunday, she and Oliver were talking, but Marie said no more than she needed to and reside in the same house. Tension still hung between them.

When it came time to clear the dishes and clean up from the meal at the Hartsell's, Oliver followed his father to the living room, although he did look at Marie before he left. She guessed he wanted to see if she would call him back.

"I can tell something is wrong," Mrs. Hartsell said as Marie washed and she dried. "Did you and Oliver have an argument?"

By now, the pressure had built in Marie, and she needed someone to talk with. None of her girlfriends would work for this, even if she'd been able to talk with them, and her parents weren't an option. "We did."

"Well, it happens to every couple eventually. You two have done really well to go this long without one."

Marie soon found herself telling Mrs. Hartsell the whole story. She didn't know if she expected the woman to side with another female over the issue or side with her son. She did neither.

"I can understand both of your positions. You want to contribute to your family's income and don't want someone controlling your choices. But Oliver wants to be the one to provide for you, and he wants to protect you."

"I just never expected this of him."

Mrs. Hartsell gave a weak smile. "He may be easy-going, but he's no pushover. My son will always do what he thinks is right. You'll have to prove him wrong before he'll change his mind."

"I just don't want to displease him, but this is important to me."

"Well, he did leave the final decision up to you,

so he's not being too controlling. You two just need to forgive each other if you feel wronged and start working together again. Marriage is hard enough without being at odds with each other. How long has this been going on?"

"We had the disagreement Thursday afternoon."

"My, oh my. That's been much too long to stay angry. My mama once told me to never go to bed angry but to talk things through if need be, and kiss and make up in any case. You need to do that, honey."

Marie nodded. She needed to do something because she couldn't stand this tension between them. It felt too much like what she'd experienced at home growing up.

"I don't like this argument we've had," Marie began as she and Oliver started home.

He glanced at her. "I don't either. Are you still planning to go to work tomorrow at the grill?"

She didn't want him to ask that for fear they'd get into another argument. "Yes, but please try to understand how important this is to me in a lot of ways."

"Why is it so important?"

She sighed. "I don't know if I can explain it because I'm not sure I've thought it all through. It's more of the feelings I have. I want to be an important part of our marriage, an equal partner, I guess. I don't want to be forced into being just a housewife because that's all my husband thinks I should be. I don't want to live the rest of my life as I have the first part, under the control and thumb of some man. I want to be able to have the final say in what I do."

He thought for a minute. "You do know that I just want the best for you. I want to protect you from any more hurt or from wearing yourself down. I'm not opposed to your working, just you working as a waitress."

"Yes, but shouldn't I be the one to decide what's best for me?"

He pulled the truck into their driveway but made no effort to get out. "I would hope we can decide together. After all, what affects you affects me, too, because we do have a partnership."

"That's why I told you as soon as you got home, but then, we just argued about it. I want to try it, and if there're problems, I'll quit."

"Okay." He reached over and took her hand. It was the first time he'd touched her since Thursday evening. "But please let me know the minute there's any problem. You can call the hardware from the grill if you need me during work."

She squeezed his hand to let him know she agreed, and she needed the friendship she felt with him. "Are we all right, then?"

"We are." He smiled, leaned over, and kissed

her cheek. "I don't ever want to argue with you again. I don't like the distance it creates between us."

"I don't either," she agreed.

He came around and helped her out of the truck, but she almost pulled away when he put his arm around her waist as they walked inside. Just because she didn't like the rift between them didn't mean she wanted to literally kiss and make up. However, she did nothing to dislodge his arm. Their relationship still felt too tenuous from the argument to do anything else to disrupt things.

Chapter Thirteen: At Work

Oliver had so many misgivings that he sat quietly in the truck Monday morning as he drove Marie to the Friendly Grill before going to the hardware. She needed to be there even earlier than he went to work.

The tension between them, which had mostly dissipated after their talk on the way home yesterday, had returned. He almost wished he'd told her he would eat at the restaurant this morning to kill some time before going to work. That way he could have seen how things went at first, and maybe that would have eased his mind some. But then, he didn't want to spend the money, not even for a cup of coffee.

"You have a good day," he told her after he'd parked the truck.

"You, too." She opened the door and climbed out before he could get around to help her.

"Oliver." Ed Thomas put his hand on the truck door to keep Marie from closing it. "Just the man I wanted to talk with. I wanted to see if I could get you to do some work for me. Come on inside so we can discuss it. I'll buy you breakfast or a cup of coffee if you've already eaten."

Oliver smiled and got out of his truck. Ed couldn't have picked a better time to want to talk.

"I need someone to replace some of the boards on the fence in the front of my property and paint the whole thing. Lisa wants it to look nice." Ed rolled his eyes as if his wife might be too picky, but he smiled with good humor, indicating he planned to please her. "Do you think you'll have time?"

"I should." Oliver tried to remember how much wooden fencing Ed had, but it didn't matter. He wouldn't turn down the job, no matter how big or small.

Mr. Little would even let him off work at the hardware when things got slow if he needed the time. However, Oliver preferred to get paid full-time at the hardware and do these jobs on the side whenever possible. He made more money that way.

"You come on by the house this afternoon, take a look, and give me a quote on what the job will cost. I already have the paint and supplies."

"I'll do that."

Ed started talking about other things, and Oliver's eyes followed Marie around the restaurant as she followed another waitress, apparently going through some sort of training. He also noticed other sets of eyes followed her, too. Marie had womanly curves that couldn't be hidden.

He clenched his fists and gritted his teeth but told himself to let it go. As long as no one tried anything, it wouldn't be too bad. What could he do anyway – go by and tell each one of them to quit looking at his wife?

"Well, I'd better get going." Ed pushed back from the table. "I just came into town to pick up some supplies, but I have a ton of things to do today." He chuckled. "If I had time, I'd fix that fence myself."

Olive took the last swallow of his coffee as he stood, too. "I need to get to work, as well." But instead of heading for the door, he turned toward Marie who had taken someone's order and headed back to the kitchen. Her training session must not have lasted long, but then Marie had always been a fast learner.

"I'll see you around three then." He kissed her cheek, hopefully letting the staring men know that she had someone watching out for her. "Mr. Little said I could leave long enough to pick you up and take you back home."

"O-okay." Her face flushed pink, and he knew he'd embarrassed her, but it couldn't be helped.

He glared at the men as he stomped out. Maybe that would give them further warning.

"How was your day?" He asked Marie when he picked her up that afternoon. She looked exhausted.

"I'm fine." She smiled and tried to put on a good front.

"Did anyone bother you?" She would know what he meant.

"No. I heard a few comments behind my back, but no one said anything to me."

"What did you hear?"

She looked out the window, and he knew she didn't want to tell him. "Don't try to keep things from me, Marie. We shouldn't keep secrets."

"One of the men told another that I looked 'knocked up' and that he'd bet you weren't the father."

They must have stared hard to figure out she's pregnant. She barely showed. "Anything else?" He suspected they'd said more.

"It's all I heard. I moved away as quickly as I could."

"Honey, I'm afraid it's only going to get worse." He made sure he kept his voice warm and tender. He had no intention of starting another argument. The first one accomplished nothing.

"I don't think so. I'm new, and that's naturally going to get extra attention. Things will be fine. What's that saying? "Sticks and stones might break my bones, but words will never hurt me."

"I hope you're right about things being fine, but words can hurt." He knew that better than most. "And in this case, words could lead to actions neither of us wants."

She shook her head. "You worry too much. Isn't that what the preacher preached on last Sunday. Just trust God and don't worry."

"But maybe God is telling us this isn't a good idea."

She gave a deep sigh. "Let's not go through this again. I know how you feel about it, and you know mine. Time will tell who's right."

He forced a smile to let her know he agreed to stop and didn't want to argue again. If time sided with him, he just prayed Marie wouldn't be hurt.

Tuesday, Mr. Austin came to the hardware. He didn't even say hello before he got right to the reason why he'd come. "What's this I hear about Marie working as a waitress at the Friendly Grill?"

"Yes, this is her second day there. She works breakfast and lunch."

"I don't like it. People are talking about her already, and now they'll think she's a wh…" He paused to look around the store. "…loose woman for sure."

"I didn't want her to work there, either, but she's adamant that's what she's going to do."

"Humph. You're the man of the house, aren't you? Put your foot down. Listen, Marie has always been headstrong, and if you let her, she'll get herself in trouble. She needs a tight rein. You'd better see to that or you'll have a wife running wild. Take care of it now." With that, the older man turned and left.

Oliver stood staring at his back. On one hand,

he'd like to make Marie listen to reason. On the other hand, he didn't want to become a hard, overbearing man like her father. *Lord, help me to do the right thing.*

He thought about not telling Marie about her father's visit, but he had been the one to say they would keep no secrets, so he told her. She shrugged it off more than he thought she would. He guessed she must be used to the man's ways, and how he acted came as no surprise.

Wednesday, they both overslept, which Oliver almost never did. "Don't pack me any lunch, he told Marie. "I'll come by the grill and get something." That way, he'd get to see her, too.

"Okay. I get my food free while I'm working and a good discount the rest of the time, so it shouldn't cost much at all."

"We probably need to get us an alarm clock," he told her as he drove toward town.

"That's something I can get with my first paycheck. And a couple of ladies that know me have asked me to make them some fall clothes. I'll have time in the afternoons after I get off work and on Saturdays. That should give us some extra income, too."

He bit his lip to keep from saying anything. Although he liked the idea of her taking in sewing much better than her working at the restaurant, he felt she should be taking things easier in her condition. Didn't she trust him to provide for them?

"You don't think working so much will be too tiring?" He did allow himself to say that much.

"No. I can sit and sew when I get home. My legs are what get tired when I'm waitressing."

The restaurant had plenty of customers when Oliver got there a little after twelve. Marie barely had time to give him a smile when he sat down. She looked harrowed, and his stomach clenched. His bill might be extra low today if he didn't feel like eating.

She delivered an order and came over to take his order. "It's good to see you, but we're busier than usual today."

"Is anything wrong?"

"I'm fine, but a few of the men who sit around and talk in the mornings seem to be getting bolder. I don't have time to talk now, but I'll tell you about it later."

He didn't want to wait, but he understood, so he nodded and gave her his order. She hurried to turn it in and bring out another tray of food.

Oliver glanced up and saw a box truck park across the street, and a burly man with a beard walked over to the grill. His swagger told what he thought of himself.

Oliver had never seen the man before, and the way his eyes scanned the place when he came in confirmed that he must be a stranger just passing through. When Marie went to take his order, his lustful look made Oliver's blood pressure rise.

"What would you like to order?" Marie asked when the man didn't say anything.

"You." His smug smile spread across his face. "I love your curves. How about meeting me in my truck in a few minutes. I can show you a better time than whoever put that baby in your belly."

"I'm married." Marie wiggled her ring finger at him. "Give me your food order or I'm leaving."

"Oh no, you're not." He grabbed Marie's arm and slung her into his lap.

Oliver was out of his seat before the man's arms got completely around her. In one motion he covered the space between them, drew back his fist, and punched the man in the side of the face, nearly knocking him out of his chair. He grabbed the table to keep from ending up on the floor. In the process, Marie became free.

"Take your hands off my wife." Oliver pulled Marie to him. As he led her to the truck, he heard Hubert Helms telling the man to leave and never return or he'd call the police. At the very least, Marie needed some time to recover, but Oliver hoped she wouldn't want to return.

Mr. Helms came out. "I'm so sorry this happened. Go ahead and take her on home. Let me know whether or not she plans to come in tomorrow. If she doesn't want to return, I'll understand. I have a couple more applicants I can call if I need to.

"I don't think I do." Marie looked about to cry.

Mr. Helms nodded. "Can't say that I blame you. I've never had anything quite like this happen before, but I guess there is a first time for everything. I'll pay you for the whole week, and you can pick up your check Friday."

Oliver put his hand over Marie's when Mr. Helms left. "Are you all right?"

"I will be. Oh, Oliver. She burst into tears. "You were right. I shouldn't have taken the job. I'm so glad you were there."

He reached over and took her in his arms. "I'm sure Mr. Helms or some of the other men there wouldn't have let anything happen to you."

"Yes, but you rescued me more quickly than they could have."

"I nearly exploded out of my chair when he pulled you into his lap. I've never been so angry in my life."

"And I've never been so scared in my life. Just take me home."

Oliver stopped by the hardware to see how busy things were and if he could take the afternoon off. He didn't want to leave Marie alone after her scare. Only one customer browsed in the store, and Mr. Little gave him the afternoon off. Oliver left with renewed appreciation that he had a job this flexible.

"I'll just concentrate on building a sewing business," Marie said as they pulled into their drive. "I like it better, anyway."

"I think that's a good idea."

"If you want to go work on that fence, I'll go and help you. I think I'd like to get of the house for a while."

"Are you sure?" Oliver tried to access how she looked. "Maybe it would better if you lay down and rested for a while."

"I'm not sleepy, and I would just lie there and think about what happened. I'd rather stay busy." Then she added, "With you."

"Okay." He pulled her into his arms and kissed her. He kept the kiss tender and not as passionate as he would have liked, but she didn't resist, and his heart soared.

Oliver loved having Marie with him as he worked. She could have helped more if he'd been ready to paint, but he needed to replace the worn boards first. Still, she handed him what he needed and helped hold the new boards in place while he nailed. The work went faster with her there, not only because of her help, but because the joy she brought made the time fly. They didn't head home until late.

"Just fix something simple for supper," he told her. "Sandwiches will be fine."

"But you didn't get to eat much of your lunch."

He smiled to let her know he didn't mind. "It doesn't matter. I can just eat an extra sandwich."

"I probably don't tell you enough, but I hope you know how much I appreciate you."

"That's good to hear." But he'd much rather hear that she loved him. *Be patient*, he told himself. That will come. Just be patient.

As Oliver rode to work the next morning, he heard Roy Orbison singing "Running Scared" on the radio. He didn't think he'd have to worry about Derrick showing up to take Marie. He felt sure she wouldn't want to leave him for someone who didn't have the decency to marry her when he got her pregnant. No, Marie would know she was his wife and honor that.

Chapter Fourteen: A Date

Marie chided herself for letting Oliver kiss her yesterday – not that it had been unpleasant – but it may have given him the wrong impression. He seemed to expect her to fall in love with him. But how could she when she loved Derrick? After what she'd done, she couldn't live with herself if she didn't love the man she'd given herself to so completely.

Oliver had been especially cheerful this morning at breakfast. No, she shouldn't have allowed him to kiss her, enjoying the moment much more than she should. Maybe her daddy had been right. Perhaps she was too wanton.

Yet, there might come a time when she needed to be a complete wife to Oliver. She might want more children than just this one. She certainly knew some of the disadvantages of growing up as an only child. However, as much as she could admire and respect Oliver, she couldn't imagine sleeping with him.

She mentally shook her head. She didn't need to jump too far ahead in her worrying. She had enough to concern her just taking one day at a time.

Today she would complete a maternity dress she had been sewing and only needed a little more work. Although she hadn't grown too large and bulky yet, no one would fail to see she was pregnant, and she could wear only a few pieces of her clothing.

After that, she would work on the two orders she had. Hopefully, when word spread, more orders would come in, especially with Christmas coming up.

She had sent two scraps of cloth with Oliver and asked him to pick up thread at Pickett's to match. "If you have trouble deciding which is best, I'm sure you can find someone there to help you," she'd told him.

After she finished her dress, she would cut out one of the orders and be ready to begin sewing when Oliver came home with the thread. She sure hoped he wouldn't forget. She almost smiled to herself. She loved to sew, and the time always flew by when she did.

She had just finished making the last stitch on her dress and started to turn the cloth to stitch back over the last few stitches before she tied the thread off when the belt snapped in two.

She looked in disbelief. It would be doubtful that anyone in town would have a belt to fit the ancient machine, and even if she could order one, it would take a while to get it in.

She closed her eyes and rested her head in her hands. So much for her plans. It looked like she wouldn't be sewing for more than a week.

Raising her head, she took a deep breath and took her dress from the machine. Using extra care since it had no backstitching, she tied off the threads. At least she had her dress finished, except for the hemming which she'd need to do by hand.

Oliver came home and immediately handed her the thread. "Did you have any trouble finding the right color?" Apparently not, unless he had help, because the thread matched the cloth perfectly.

"No. This looked about as close as one could get." His eyes grew wary. "Is it all right?"

"Oh, yes," she quickly reassured him. "It's exactly what I needed."

"Then what's wrong?" Did he know her that well or was he just especially observant?

"The belt on the sewing machine broke, and I don't know if we can get another or not."

"Let me have a look. Maybe I can fix it."

She hadn't thought of that, but she led him to her bedroom with renewed hope. If he could get it working until she could get a new one, that would be great.

"Thank you," she said when he'd finished. "You're a life saver. I didn't want to have to wait for who knows how long to get a belt that would fit."

He beamed. "I'm glad I could help. I measured the belt and will see if we can order one that will fit. If we can no longer order one from Singer, maybe another one will work."

"Thank you," she repeated. "You've made my day." Before she thought, she leaned over and brushed a kiss across his lips.

How stupid could she get? After just admonishing herself for letting him kiss her, now she goes and kisses him. She tried to tell herself that this peck didn't compare with the kiss he had given her, but the smile that spread across his face told he enjoyed it anyway.

"I like making you happy," he said, looking at her lips with longing.

She turned away before she did something even more stupid. "I'll go get supper ready. I have most of it done."

Friday, Marie sewed most of the day, and her back began to cramp and hurt. She tried to put a cushion at her back, but it didn't help. Despite how much she liked to sew, she found herself exhausted by the time Oliver got home.

"Is something wrong?" He put his lunchbox down and came to her.

"My back is just hurting, and I'm tired from sewing all day."

"Honey, you need to take it easier. You don't have to do so much all at once. You need to take plenty of breaks and rest along. You should even consider taking an afternoon nap."

would. Where her father had only wanted to be served food he'd grown accustomed to, now she could prepare some of the recipes she'd learned in home economics and ones she found in magazines. She especially liked to cook new things.

This is really good." Oliver looked at her from across the table. "What's it called?"

"It's just a chicken casserole." She liked recipes that made the meat go farther or could be fixed from leftovers. I have an oven now, so I can cook more of a variety."

She thought he would take her comment as a compliment, but his face fell. "I'm sorry that I've not been able to get everything we need right away. If we had been able to date and then have a longer engagement, I could have saved and been better prepared."

Would she have dated him if he'd asked before Derrick? Probably, but her father likely wouldn't have allowed it. Before she became pregnant, he'd expected her to marry well.

"That's okay. I understand." And she did. Oliver had been trying to help his family while he lived with them. "We're doing fine. Many young couples struggle financially at first."

His eyes told her he appreciated what she said, but Marie couldn't help but recall how well-off Derrick seemed to be. She got up to get them some more tea to prevent Oliver from reading any expression she might have. He had an uncanny ability to read her mind sometimes.

Oliver finished the repairs on the fence. Marie thought he needed help to paint it, but he disagreed.

"I'm afraid the paint fumes might not be good for you and the baby," he said.

"I might agree if we were painting inside, but I don't think it'll be a problem outside where there's plenty of fresh air."

"I'm not sure I want to take that chance." Stubborn man.

"I have a doctor's appointment tomorrow. We'll ask Dr. McCloud."

"Okay." He had already said he wanted to go with her to all her doctor's appointments.

"As long as she doesn't experience any unusual symptoms, it should be fine," the doctor told them. "Everything looks normal and the days have gotten a lot cooler, so the heat shouldn't be a problem."

Oliver relaxed. He must have been more worried about Marie than he realized.

However, he still planned to enlist the help of

some of his brothers to paint the fence, so Marie wouldn't be painting as long. He would pay them with some treat, maybe even one of Marie's special meals. Although Mom cooked delicious meals, her fare didn't vary much and tended to have a lot of dried beans and things that didn't cost much to prepare, except for special occasions and sometimes Sunday dinners. Dad had most of the harvest in now and could spare a couple of the younger Hartsells.

His youngest brothers and sisters were filled with excitement when they went to his family's for Sunday dinner. The elementary school had scheduled a fall festival for the last Friday evening in October.

"You've got to come," Jenny said. "It'll be so much fun."

Oliver looked at Marie for an answer. She looked undecided and said, "Let's talk about it later."

He nodded. A part of him wanted to go. As things stood, he was just courting Marie, and this would be a good date. However, the activities would require some money because the school did this as a fundraiser, but he guessed they could do more looking around than participating.

"So, what do you think about the fall festival?" Oliver asked when they were on their way home.

"I'm not sure I want to be in the crowd. It will seem more crowded than the Fourth of July because we will all be in a more confined space."

He looked at her more carefully. Was she not feeling well? Did he need to take her back to the doctor?

"Besides, I don't look forward to everyone gawking at my big belly."

He realized this was her real reason for not wanting to go. "You are married now. Their stares shouldn't cause you any discomfort. Besides, you look wonderful."

She gave a laugh that held little amusement. "You should try being pregnant and then you would see discomfort."

Now would be a good time to hush. He had heard of women being moody during pregnancies, but he hadn't seen it in Marie before.

They didn't go to the fall festival, but Oliver splurged and took Marie to a movie in Albemarle. He rationalized that it cost no more than he would have spent at the school had they gone.

"It's a shame the theater in Oakboro burned or that it wasn't built back," Marie said on their way to Albemarle.

"I agree, but I don't think it made enough money near the end to warrant spending money on building a new one."

The Center Theater was playing *West Side*

Story. Marie liked the movie, but neither of them liked the ending. Oliver looked at Marie, hoping their story turned out better. He didn't know if he could handle a tragedy in real life.

At least he had been able to hold her hand after they have finished sharing a tub of popcorn. That made the movie worth seeing for him.

"Thank you for taking me to a movie," Marie told him as they walked back to the truck.

He managed to slip his arm around her on the pretext of keeping her warm in the chilly night. "You're welcome. I enjoyed it, too." He enjoyed being with her like this.

She leaned her head on his shoulder for a few seconds as they walked. The affectionate gesture made him want to take her in his arms and kiss her until she saw stars.

When they got to the truck, she scooted close to him on the bench seat. If taking her to a romantic movie got this type of reaction, he wished he could afford to bring her more often. However, he hoped the movie wasn't the only reason she moved closer to him. Dare he hope that she had begun to fall in love with him?

Chapter Fifteen: Vehicles

Marie awoke Saturday morning with the warm feeling of the night before still surrounding her. She felt as if she and Oliver had been on a real date. When she'd lived with her parents, she never got to do much, so going to the theater felt special.

She liked the movie, although she hadn't liked the ending. But the acting had been good, and she enjoyed the music and the dancing, as well as the love story.

And she could admit to herself that she liked being with Oliver. Always kind and considerate, he made a good companion. She felt safe and comfortable with him.

"It looks like today is going to be a pretty day," Oliver said at breakfast. "Since I don't have any jobs lined up, why don't we take a picnic lunch to Morrow Mountain. With the weather growing cooler, we won't have many more days left this year when we'll be able to spend much time relaxing outdoors."

Marie had all her sewing nearly finished. She just needed to do the handwork on one. "I'd like that."

She didn't want to let go of the special feeling last night had given her, and maybe Oliver felt the same way. He had become her best friend, and she liked spending time with him, especially when they could enjoy the time and not be busy with work.

They hiked the trails first. Oliver didn't want to take the longest, steepest trail with her expecting, but the one they took turned out to be taxing enough. Perhaps she had been sitting in front of the sewing machine too much lately.

They walked at a moderate pace, not pushing themselves but faster than a stroll. Still, Oliver either put his arm around her or held her hand. She told herself she liked him doing that so much because it gave her a sense of security.

"Maybe we can come back in the summer when the swimming pool is open," Marie said when they drove to the picnic area across from the pool area. With only a few others here today, they almost had the area to themselves.

Oliver grinned. "We'll plan on it. I'd like to see you in a swimsuit."

Marie felt the heat climbing up her face, despite the cooler temperatures. Her embarrassment came, not only from the idea of him wanting to see more of her, but also from the fact that he was her husband and never had.

They watched the antics of the squirrels playing in and around the oak trees as they ate. Marie envied their carefree happiness. But when she looked at Oliver, she didn't have much to complain about. Things could have turned out a whole lot worse.

After they finished a leisurely lunch, they looked around some more and visited the small museum. They left the park a little after three. On the way out, a magnificent, large buck ran across their path.

"Do you hunt?" She thought she knew the answer, but sometimes she couldn't understand why anyone would want to kill such a beautiful animal."

"I do, but only to use the meat. I would never hunt for trophy heads as some do. With plenty of men in the family, we keep Mom's freezer well-stocked. It sure helps out."

"I can understand that much better than I can hunting just to have the heads mounted and hung on the wall. Will you hunt this year, since we don't have a freezer big enough for a whole deer?"

"I might try to get one. We'll put what we can in our freezer on the refrigerator and give Mom the rest. We usually eat there at least once a week, anyway. If they needed it, I would go out more, but Dad and the boys like to hunt, too."

She nodded. She had never been opposed to hunting. She guessed the sight of that beautiful creature made her more sensitive than usual about it.

When they went to pick up the rest of the Hartsells for church Sunday, another pickup sat in the drive. Although still old, it was newer than the one

Oliver usually drove.

"Who's here."

Oliver stared at the unfamiliar truck. "I don't know. I don't recognize that vehicle."

Oliver's father came out before they got their doors opened. "I would have called you if I could have, but we won't have to crowd up in one truck today. A man I've helped out some gave me a deal on this truck, and I can pay him back over the next two years without interest."

"That sounds good." Oliver's eyes were on the newer truck. I'll come take a look."

Marie guessed he wanted to have a closer look and open the hood for inspection. She wondered if they'd have time without being late for Sunday School.

But Mr. Hartsell stopped his son. "We're all ready to go. Why don't you wait, and we'll have more time after church when you come back for dinner?"

Oliver nodded, restarted the truck, and turned around. "I'm glad Dad could get the second truck. I know he's needed a vehicle sometimes when I had the truck at the hardware, and it's not good for the family to be without one for as long as they have. Even getting their groceries has to be scheduled and planned."

"I agree." She knew all this firsthand. She had never had as much as the other girls because her Dad didn't think she needed them, but the Hartsells didn't have because they couldn't afford them.

When they got back to Hartsells, Oliver and his father stayed outside to look at the new truck while Marie went inside to help Mrs. Hartsell get Sunday dinner on the table.

Oliver came straight to her when they came in. "Dad has given us the old truck. We're going to transfer the title tomorrow. I'll just have to pay the insurance and taxes, which shouldn't be too much."

"That's good." She didn't feel as excited as Oliver looked, but it would be good to have transportation of their own without having to coordinate and share. Like Oliver, she knew the Hartsells had sacrificed so he could have the truck most of the time.

They'd been putting off lighting the woodstove in the living room, but Oliver started it the next morning. "We'll just knock the chill off. If it warms up in the day, you can let it die down."

Oliver's father and brothers had been cutting wood for winter, but Oliver had only gone with them a couple of times. However, Mr. Hartsell had still shared with them and said they could get more anytime they needed it.

By Thanksgiving, Marie felt like a lead balloon,

round and heavy, and she still had three months to go. She went to the Hartsells for dinner vowing that she wouldn't eat much. However, everything tasted so good she felt even more stuffed when she got up from the table.

She saw Oliver slip his mother some money to help with the meal. A part of her wished he wouldn't do that since they still needed so much, but another part wanted to help this poor family who had been more than generous with them.

She closed her eyes in regret that her father, who could afford to do so much, had done very little. He'd just let them live in a shabby little house that they had to fix up at their own expense. She took a deep breath.

Forgive me, Lord. I have much to be thankful for on this day of Thanksgiving. Help me to focus on what I do have and not what I don't.

She opened her eyes to see Oliver looking at her. He gave her an encouraging smile, even though he had no idea what she'd been thinking.

Whatever bothered her, he wanted to take care of and lend his support. He had become one of her many blessings, and she needed to remember that.

As always, Christmas followed close on Thanksgiving's heels. Marie worked hard to make her presents. She made her mother an apron and hemmed some white squares to make her father some handkerchiefs. Those didn't take long, but she wanted to have them something, whether or not they got her anything. If Mama had her way, they might.

She made each of the males in Hartsell family a shirt and each of the females a blouse. With such a large family, that took more time. However, she would need to spend the most time on Oliver's gifts. She planned to sew two shirts and a set of handkerchiefs for him and also knit him a sweater and two pairs of heavy socks for winter.

She took Oliver to work and kept the truck to buy what she needed for the gifts. She went to Pickett's, looking forward to browsing through the material until her heart's content. Being by herself, she wouldn't feel the need to hurry. Although Oliver had never rushed her, she didn't want to dawdle while he waited.

She had just checked out and exited the store when Derrick suddenly appeared. Her heart started beating a fast tempo.

"I have my car parked off the main street, so let's go there and talk. I don't think anyone will notice us if that concerns you." He took her by the elbow, almost pushing her along.

She pulled back. "Let me put this big bag in the truck. It's parked right here."

He stood back and allowed her to do that, but

then put his hand on her back, propelling her along again. She wondered about the wisdom of going with him.

He didn't really give her a choice, however, although she guessed she could have jerked away. However, it was good to see him again after such a long time, and she wondered what he wanted. He looked even better than she remembered.

He opened the car door for her, something that he hadn't always done, and helped her down into the low sports car. "It's a good thing the seat is all the way back. You sure have gotten big."

He closed her door and went around to get in the driver's side. "But you still look good." He kept his eyes focused on her face.

"What did you want?" Sitting in his car like this didn't feel right, and she felt an urge to get out.

"Just to see you, to see how you're doing. I tried to stay away, but I couldn't."

Her heart softened at his words. "I've missed you, too." It was true but not as true as it had been in the beginning.

"And I wanted to give you this." He reached into the center console, pulled out a box wrapped in Christmas paper, and handed it to her.

She set it in her lap and looked at it. She hadn't gotten him anything, having no idea that she'd even see him. And no matter how well-made it was, she doubted if he would wear a homemade shirt.

"Well, go ahead and open it."

She did as he said, but she could tell the fact that she didn't enthusiastically rip into it displeased him. She took out a beautiful three-strand necklace. The small turquoise beads were twisted together and had an expensive look about them.

"It's gorgeous, but I can't accept this." She lay it back into the box and dared to look at him.

As she expected, he scowled. "Why not?"

"I'd never get to wear it. How would I explain such a thing? And I won't lie about it."

"I thought about getting you some red lingerie, but I couldn't stand the thoughts that Oliver might get to see you in them instead of me."

Was he trying to hurt her now because she had refused his gift? Surely, he couldn't be serious about wanting to give her lingerie. She had an idea of how revealing it would be if he picked it out.

She needed to get away. "Thank you for the thought, Derrick. That's what counts, and I love you for it, but I need to go. "I'm supposed to meet Oliver for lunch."

He looked somewhat placated, but his face fell at the mention of Oliver. "I had hoped you would eat lunch with me and then maybe we could spend some special time together."

"I'm sorry, but I need to go." She opened her

door and got out, leaving the box with the necklace on the seat, before he could say anything else. This hadn't been a good idea, and she certainly didn't want to eat lunch with him where anyone could see them. Thankfully, he didn't try to follow her.

To her dismay, her hands were shaking as she got in and tried to start the truck. She sat there a few minutes to calm herself. She'd need to get a handle on her emotions before she picked up Oliver. If she remained the least bit upset, he would notice and want to know what had happened.

Her few minutes with Derrick had churned her emotions, and she didn't enjoy eating out with Oliver the way she expected. They rarely spent the money to go to a restaurant, and this should have been a rare treat. As it turned out, she could hardly look Oliver in the eyes, and her appetite had fled.

"Aren't you feeling well?" Oliver put his hand over hers in concern.

She shook her head. Seeing Derrick had stirred up old feelings, and she didn't feel well. She still loved him, but something about him bothered her more than it used to. She felt confused and unsettled.

"Do you need to go to the doctor?"

Even Oliver's worry over her struck her the wrong way. Why couldn't he just back off and give her some space? His hovering didn't set well.

"No, I'll be fine. I'll lie down and rest after you

take me home before I start on my sewing."

"You were probably on your feet too long with your shopping. Can you eat, or do you want me to get you a to-go box and take you home now?"

"I'll eat with you." She took a bite of her sandwich to prove her point.

"I've never seen such a playboy," Marie heard two middle-aged women in the booth behind her talking.

She had noticed them before she sat down, but she didn't know them well. She thought she had seen them before but couldn't recall their names.

"He might have a handsome face, but 'handsome is as handsome does,'" my mother always said."

"I heard he got that girl in Norwood pregnant and paid for her to have an abortion, and from what I understand that's not the first and probably won't be the last.

"You don't say. I wonder if he's not the father of the Austin girl's baby then. I never did think it would likely be Oliver Hartsell, even though he did marry her. I think Mary Jane told me she went to the Albemarle prom with Derrick."

Marie barely kept from gasping out loud. They were talking about her.

"I heard that, too. I guess it could be either Oliver or Derrick. I don't think she's ever dated anyone else. Her father tried to keep a tight rein on her. I used to think he was being too harsh, but I guess he knew things we didn't."

Marie looked at Oliver to see if he'd heard what the women had said, but he showed no signs of it. Either their voices hadn't carried across the booth to him, or his mind had been preoccupied with something else.

She pushed her half-eaten sandwich toward him. "You finish this. I've had all I want."

He looked startled, and she guessed she had pulled him back into the present. "Are you sure. You could take it with you to eat later."

"No, you eat it. I won't want anything else until supper."

Over the following days, Marie managed to fit back into their routine. Yet, although she tried to keep stray thoughts a bay, they crept back in at odd times.

Apparently, the women hadn't seen Oliver and her come in. They were likely too busy gossiping. And she wondered if Mary Jane was related to one of them, but her friend shouldn't be talking about her and giving out information, regardless.

More disturbing, was what they said about Derrick true? Had he gotten other girls pregnant? She ran back through what she knew of him and how he'd treated her. No, she couldn't believe that of him. She'd be wise not to listen to malicious gossip, which was usually highly exaggerated if not totally fabricated.

She tried to lose herself in her sewing, but much of the routine tasks gave her too much time to think. Even Oliver mentioned how preoccupied she seemed, but she brushed it off as being due to the coming holidays.

Christmas came. She and Oliver decided to exchange their presents on Christmas morning before they went to his parents' house.

They had a cedar Christmas tree Oliver had cut from his family's farm, and Marie had made the decorations. She had wrapped the clothes she had made Oliver in one big box, and he had a small one for her under the tree. With the presents for the rest of his family, it looked and smelled like Christmas.

She loved the smell of the cedar tree, but she didn't like its prickly needles, and its shape didn't look quite as nice as a fir or spruce. Those were way too expensive to buy, however, and an artificial tree, as well.

Marie made coffee first thing Christmas morning, but Oliver wanted to open their presents before breakfast. He seemed as excited as a small child, but more so about what he'd gotten her than his.

He handed her the one with her name on it and scooted his large one with his foot toward where he would sit. She had shaken hers already, and it felt awfully light, but she could hear the faint sound of something moving inside.

"I'll open mine first," he told her.

She looked at him in surprise. Normally, he would have wanted her to go first.

She didn't need to respond for he tore into his quickly, pulling each item out and exclaiming over it. She breathed a sigh of relief and relaxed. She could tell he liked everything.

"This is too much." He looked up at her with pleasure written all over his face. "You shouldn't have spent so much time on me, but I do love it all."

She had worked hard to get everything finished while he worked, but she had enjoyed doing it. And his joy made it all worth it.

"Now open yours." The gleam in his eyes made her curious.

She opened her box to find a single white card which read, "Your present was too big to wrap. If you will go to your room and not look out, I will go get it."

He laughed at the questioning look she gave him. "Go on now and stay there until I come get you."

He must have gotten her something like a large puppy. She would like to have a dog, but she would have preferred to wait until after the baby grew some. However, she wouldn't tell Oliver that and ruin his present.

He came back grinning and led her to the front door. "Now close your eyes and no peeking. I'll lead you outside and then tell you when you can open your eyes."

He sure was making a big production out of this, but she did what he said, wanting to please him. However, she couldn't imagine doing this for a puppy, but what else could it be?

"Okay, open your eyes."

She did, but the image blurred in front of her. She blinked hard. What in the world? She looked at him in wonder, wanting him to assure her that this was indeed her Christmas present.

Chapter Sixteen: Christmas and the New Year

"Do you like it?" The look on Marie's face told Oliver she did. "Come on and have a look."

She looked from him back to the car, and he followed her gaze. The metallic pink Chevrolet wasn't new, but it looked much newer than Oliver's old truck.

"How could you afford this?" She seemed to say the first thing that came to her mind, but he expected the question.

"The bank got it back as a repossession and couldn't sell it. I don't know if it was because of the unusual color or something else. Your father bought it, and I'm going to pay him back by working for him."

She frowned. "He'll require you to work hard for every penny and beyond."

"That's okay. I have what I need to do in writing from him. I'm to take care of his cattle through the winter, repair the barn, and fix a few things in the house. He's going to buy all the materials needed, so we don't have to worry about that. I know he didn't pay much for the car, but that's all right. It's worth it to me to do the work so you can have a car. I know your father is coming out ahead on the deal, but I couldn't pass the offer up."

"Thank you!" She jumped into his arms for a

quick sideways hug. "I love it!"

He chuckled. "Now, there's the reaction I was hoping for."

She ran to the car and sat in the driver's side, running her hand over the interior. "May I drive it to your parent's house?"

"You sure can and to church Sunday, too."

Oliver couldn't describe how much her excitement and joy affected him. He felt fulfilled, as if maybe he could be the husband she wanted and needed. There had been so many things he wanted to give her and couldn't, but this one unexpected and maybe even a bit extravagant present almost seemed to make up for some of it.

Her face became pinker than the car when she had to work to adjust her seat to fit her belly behind the steering wheel. "This will be easier after the baby comes."

"It won't be long now, will it? Less than two months."

"I can't wait to get back to a normal weight and be able to get comfortable again, but I also dread going through the labor pains."

He reached over for her hand since he didn't know what to say. He dreaded the thoughts of her experiencing the labor process and had been praying hard for her and the baby. He, too, would be glad when it was all over if everything turned out okay.

She squeezed his hand. "I hope you know how much I appreciate your support and care. You have gone to my doctor's appointments and been considerate and supportive. I would have been lost without you."

"I love you, Marie." The words came out as if they had a mind of their own. He had thought it often, but he hesitated to say it.

She'd even told him she would never love him, but she hadn't said it lately. He let out the breath he'd been holding when she didn't repeat it now. She appreciated him, and he'd consider that a step in the right direction.

She gave him a quick glance as she put the car in reverse. "I'd like to drop a couple of small presents by my parents' house if that's okay."

"Of course. I expected you'd want to see them sometime today." He noticed, however, that she didn't look excited about the prospect.

"Consider me telling Oliver about the car as my present to you," her father said when Marie handed him his present.

Her mother walked them to the door. "I have some of your old baby things set aside in the attic – a bassinet and such. Come by and get them sometime when your father's at work," she whispered.

Their time at his parents' house seemed almost as hectic as he had remembered in the past. Santa Claus had already come for the youngest children, bringing them each one gift and filling their Christmas stocking with goodies, so that lessened the chaos a little. But they'd waited for him and Marie to open their presents from each other, all of which turned out to be handmade like usual.

"Oh, I love it!" Marie exclaimed when she opened the white trash bag with a red yarn tie and took out a quilt his mom had made. She rubbed her hand over it. "I know how much time and effort something like this takes. Thank you so much!"

"It's the double wedding ring pattern for both of you." His mom looked between Oliver and Marie. "It's supposed to ensure happiness for the couple who sleeps under it."

Marie dropped her eyes as color crawled up her neck into her face. Oliver would pay a pretty penny to know her thoughts. Did she regret that they had waited so long, or did the thought of sleeping with him repulse her? He could see nothing in her face, except embarrassment.

Everyone seemed happy with the gifts Marie and made them. This family could always use anything to eat or wear.

"You put an awful lot of work into making all these presents," his mother told her. "But your sewing is lovely, some of the best I've ever seen. No wonder you're getting plenty of orders."

Marie didn't say anything, but she beamed at the praise. He didn't think she'd ever had much from her parents.

"She made my sweater, too." Oliver looked down at the forest green sweater with the neck, sleeves, and waist edged with a narrow white line.

"Why, I thought you'd bought that at Belk or somewhere. It's a mighty fine-looking sweater, and it looks good on you, son."

Mom had cooked a ham for dinner with too many side dishes to name. Marie had baked a lemon pie, his favorite, to bring, and Oliver ate until he felt he might pop.

They sat around and talked for a while after all the dishes were done. When he looked up and saw how heavy Marie's eyes looked, he stood. "I think it's time for us to head home. Marie needs to rest, and to be honest, I think I could use a nap after that big meal."

The older boys snickered until Dad gave them a cut-it-out glare. Oliver could overlook their silliness, but he didn't want them to embarrass Marie.

"I really like your car, Marie." Dad got up to walk out with them. "The boys and I looked it over while you were helping Louise get the food set out. Oliver did all right."

She smiled, first at his father and then her smile

widened when she looked at Oliver. "I think so, too. It's a wonderful gift and one I didn't even think possible."

Oliver hadn't mentioned that he would have to watch their money to be able to pay the insurance. However, he'd made his wife radiantly happy, and he'd scrimp and take on as many extra jobs as he could to keep her that way.

That night, Oliver and Marie sat on the small, used loveseat they had in the living room and sipped hot chocolate while they listened to Christmas music and looked at their Christmas tree.

He stretched out his arm behind her, more on the back of the sofa than on her, but he felt at peace. She gave a contented sigh, and he moved his arm the few inches to her shoulders.

"It's been a good Christmas, hasn't it?" She leaned her head sideways and let it rest on his shoulder.

He gently kissed the top of her head. "Yes, it certainly has." He'd take more days just like it. It would have been even better if he could have kissed her or if he could take her to bed in a few minutes, but he'd be thankful for the progress he saw.

Hm-m-m. Kissing her. Did he dare? He moved just enough that he could see her lips.

She looked up at him but didn't pull away. He

put his arms around her at an angle to compensate for her bulge and lowered his head slowly to give her time to move if she felt the need. She stayed fixed in place.

When his lips were close to hers, she closed her eyes. He needed no other invitation.

An explosive fire melted his body to lava, but it felt wonderful instead of unpleasant. As the kiss intensified, he felt her lips move against his, her body flow into him, her essence surround him. He was drowning in her, but he only wanted more.

She pulled away first, but she moved slowly as if she also needed time to recover. And instead of leaving his arms entirely, she repositioned and lay her head back on his shoulder.

He tugged her a little closer. "That was too fantastic for words. I can't even begin to describe it."

She didn't say anything, but he felt her nod against his shoulder. Dare he hope she felt too overwhelmed for words? His heart ached with love.

After Christmas, they remained close, as if they'd taken giant steps forward to stay in tune with each other. He expected things would be even more right after the baby came and Marie had time to recover. He looked forward to that time with eager anticipation and joy.

He hadn't tried to do more than kiss the back of her hand, cheek, or forehead since Christmas night. It had been hard enough to live in the same house with the woman he loved and not have a physical relationship. With many more kisses like that, he didn't think he could control himself, but there were only about two months left. He had waited five months; he could wait for two more.

The one exception to his resolution came on New Year's Eve. Mary Jane had sent them an invitation to her party to ring in the new year. However, Marie decided she didn't want to go. He hoped it wasn't because of him, but he knew she felt uncomfortable with her bulky middle now, and she had grown apart from her former friends when she found they gossiped about her.

They didn't have a television to watch – maybe next year for Christmas if all went well – but he found a station playing Guy Lombardo's New Year Eve's Party on the old radio.

Marie talked him into dancing with her, but they did it in reverse. He stood behind her, put his arms around her above her bulge, and they swayed to the music. He had never had any practice at dancing, but the fact that she wanted to dance with him thrilled him, and he didn't find swaying like this difficult. He liked the way she leaned back against him.

At midnight the bells rang, and he did kiss her again, a kiss just as potent as the last one, maybe even more so. He thought it might have lasted longer and been even more intense, but he couldn't be sure. Time moved to a whole other dimension when he kissed her like this.

A snowstorm hit toward the end of January. Most of the downtown stores were closed, and Oliver and Marie stayed in the house the first day due to the almost blizzard-like conditions. However, the next day dawned clearer, the snow had stopped, and the temperatures hovered in the low thirties.

"Let's go outside," Marie said after breakfast. "I'd love to play in the snow."

"Are you sure you feel up to it?" He knew she'd gotten more uncomfortable as her time neared.

"I would like to try it. I can always come back inside."

"I'm not sure that's wise." He could imagine her sliding down in her off-balanced state.

"Don't be such a mother hen," she teased. "I'll be careful, and you'll be right beside me."

They bundled up and went outside. The snow hadn't frozen over, so it was still powdery and not as slick as it could have been.

Marie wanted to make a snowman first, and he helped her work on it for the first hour. Their life-size creation didn't look half bad.

"I would love to make snow angels." She laughed. "But once I got down, I'm afraid it would be too hard to get up."

He could have pulled her up, but he didn't encourage her. However, he did find himself lying on the ground, flapping in the snow, and making snow angels for her.

She made a couple of snowballs and threw them at him, but he didn't reciprocate. No way would he hit a pregnant woman with a snowball.

After spending about two hours outside, they went inside to fix some soup for lunch. He loved her homemade soups.

Marie couldn't wipe the grin off her face as they went inside from playing in the snow. She had been able to do more than she expected, which went to show that desire made a big difference in accomplishing something.

Her grin fell away. Thinking of desire led her mind to places she'd tried to avoid. She had reluctantly let Oliver kiss her Christmas night because the day had gone so well, and she had warmed to him in their quiet moment together on the loveseat.

That kiss, though, had taken her completely by surprise. She enjoyed it more than she dared admit.

Therefore, when New Year's Eve came, she wanted him to kiss her – looked forward to it, in fact.

Derrick had also turned her on, but it was hard to remember and compare how much. Did that make her a floozy? She didn't understand herself sometimes.

She tried to tell herself she just wanted to make sure Oliver's kisses would be everything she remembered. Maybe it had been a one-time thing, but it hadn't been. The kiss on New Year's Eve melted her even more than the one at Christmas. There was a lot more to Oliver than she'd ever thought.

She had even talked him into dancing with her. Having his arms wrapped around her, and feeling his body at her back, pressed against her and moving with hers, made her thoughts go to places it shouldn't. She must be turning into a loose woman, and she hated herself for it.

What should she do? In her confusion, she decided to do nothing. She would let Oliver call the shots. He had promised to wait until after the baby came to sleep with her, and she knew he would do what he said. Hopefully, the few remaining weeks would give her time to work it all out in her mind.

She finally drove to see her mother. She had put it off long enough. She went right before Oliver would get off from work, and he would meet her there to carry the bassinet and haul it in the truck. She went early to see if there was anything else in the attic she could use.

"It's so good to see you." Her mother gave her a tentative hug. "I've missed you."

Marie wondered if Mama missed her or all the work she used to do here. She had less to do keeping house for Oliver.

But giving her the benefit of a doubt, she hugged her mother back. Mama had always been warmer than Daddy, although neither one of them would kindle a fire in that area.

She didn't stay long after Oliver came. They loaded up the bassinet, a playpen, and two boxes of baby things. This, along with the baby shower the church had given them, would help.

A letter came for Oliver that had a return address from some lawyer in Salisbury. Marie stood back and watched him open it with as much curiosity as he looked to have.

"Oh, my!"

She went closer to see what the letter contained. He looked up at her in wonder. "Some great aunt I don't even remember died and left me her estate. She lived in an apartment, so there won't be much property, but we can have any of the furnishings we want, and she had nearly ten thousand dollars in savings."

"That's wonderful."

"I just need to go meet with the lawyer at my earliest convenience, show identification, and sign some papers. I'll call tomorrow from the hardware and get an appointment." He looked up with his eyes shining with excitement. "Now we won't have to scrimp so much, and we can give the baby the home it deserves." His eyes told her he could give her more, too. Leave it to Oliver to think of what he could give her and the baby and not what he could buy for himself.

Chapter Seventeen: The Birth

In February, Marie said she just wanted to have the baby's birth over with, and she couldn't wait to get her body back to a more normal size. Oliver looked forward to that, too, but he didn't say so. Things between them had been going so well he didn't want to say or do anything that might cause Marie to pull back.

Early Monday morning, Oliver heard Marie moving around. He looked at the clock. One-thirty. Maybe she had just gotten up to use the bathroom. He listened carefully and kept hearing faint sounds. He'd better get up to check on her.

He tapped on her bedroom door. "Marie, is everything all right?"

"Yes, come in."

When he opened the door, she grimaced and held her abdomen. Everything didn't look all right to him. "Is it time?" He noticed that she had dressed.

"I think so." She moved to pick up the bag she'd packed at the first of the month.

He grabbed it before she could, but his hand trembled as he picked it up. Wasn't this too early – two weeks before the doctor figured her due date. He glanced at the calendar she had hung above her sewing machine. And two days before Valentine's Day.

"Are you ready?" Did his voice tremble? "It's a long drive to Albemarle."

She gave him a nervous smile. "Not that long."

She reached back for her coat she'd laid across the foot of her bed. He should be helping more. He put the bag on the floor and helped her into her coat. "How do you feel?"

"Ready to get this over with." She looked at him with almost pleading eyes. "But I'm also nervous and a little scared."

He knew how that felt. He gave her a quick hug, picked up the bag, and gently pushed her toward the door. "Let's get you to the hospital then."

"Get your coat."

"Oh, yeah." He thought about just going without it, but that probably wouldn't be wise. He rushed to get it.

He helped her into the car and got in himself. His hand trembled even more when he tried to put the key into the ignition. He should have come out and warmed up the car for her, but did he have time?"

Well, it was too late to worry about that. He needed to concentrate on getting her to the hospital safely. He prayed as they started off. He had a feeling he would fill any waiting with lots of prayers.

They got Marie checked in, and he stayed with her at first, but when they wheeled her back to the maternity ward, he was told to go into the waiting room. He managed to brush his lips against her cheek and whisper he loved her before they whisked her away.

He scrubbed a hand down his face, rough with stubble. He didn't feel like sitting, but no one else occupied the waiting room, so he stood and moved around some. The room wasn't tiny, but he wished it were larger. He didn't have enough room to pace as he'd like.

A nurse looked in. "Your wife has only dilated to a three, so it will likely be a while yet. Someone will let you know when anything important happens."

He peeked outside and looked at the clock over the nurses' station. A little before three. Since it might take a while, he would wait until his parents would likely be up to call them, and they could call Marie's parents. At least, his parents had gotten a phone for their Christmas present to each other.

He went to a pay phone and called his parents when the clock showed seven. His mom answered. "We'll be over as soon as the kids are off to school."

"Would you call Marie's parents and anyone else you think should know?"

"Sure. I can do that."

His parents came at seven-thirty, and he was glad to see them. He needed some diversion besides clock-watching. Its hands moved way too slowly.

"I can't understand what's taking so long. It's already been over five hours." He didn't try to hide his nervous impatience. Those five hours felt more like fifty.

His mother patted his shoulder. "Birthing usually takes a while, especially with the first one. You've likely got another five hours."

He didn't want to hear that news. How would he survive?

"Here." Mom reached into her purse and pulled out a small paper bag. "I brought you two egg and sausage biscuits. I bet you haven't eaten breakfast."

"I haven't even thought about food." He took the bag, wondering if his unsettled stomach came from hunger or worry.

"You'd better eat up." His father's grin told that he would be teasing. "You'll need all the strength you can muster to get up with a crying infant multiple times a night. Believe me, I speak from plenty of experience."

Oliver's smile probably looked weak and uncertain, but he managed one anyway. If he and Marie could just get through this and take a healthy baby home, he wouldn't complain about any loss of sleep.

He bought a cup of coffee from the machine. It didn't taste nearly as good as Marie's did. Taking one of the biscuits out of the bag, he began to nibble on it.

"I called the Austins, and Mr. Austin answered the phone." His mother shifted in her seat. "He said they might come by after supper, but he had to work today. He also said to let them know if there were any problems or whether it was a girl or a boy."

Oliver gritted his teeth. He couldn't imagine such parents.

About ten, the doctor came to talk with him. "Your wife has dilated to a four and seems stuck there, so this has turned into a waiting game. She is doing fine and has even slept a little. She isn't in hard labor, but the nurses are keeping a close check on her. This is unusual, but nothing to be too concerned about. We'll give her a while longer, and if there's no progress, we can consider a Caesarean section."

"Operate?" The word almost stuck in Oliver's throat.

"Yes, but not to worry. It's a common one with little risk."

Not to worry? Easy for him to say. "May I see her?" If he could just see for himself, he would feel much better.

The doctor shook his head. "No, I'm sorry. We keep everything back there as sterile as possible. I'm sure you wouldn't want to take anything back that could potentially harm Marie or the baby."

Oliver gulped down his disappointment and nodded. "How much longer do you think it'll be."

"No way to tell at this point. We'll keep you informed." With that, he left.

"Well, I need to go get some work done." His dad stood. "Are you coming, Louise, or are you going to stay here?"

She looked at Oliver as if trying to determine if he needed her and then looked back at her husband. "If you can fix you a sandwich or something for lunch, I'll stay here."

His dad nodded, kissed his wife on the cheek. "I'll come back this afternoon, as soon as I get a few things done but definitely before the kids get home from school."

Mom tried to talk with him, but Oliver couldn't keep his mind on anything besides Marie long enough to carry on much conversation. She finally gave up and sat in silence.

Oliver tried to sit with her, but he ended up moving around a lot. "Maybe you should have gone home with Dad," he finally told her, "but I do appreciate you staying with me, although I know I'm not much company."

She patted his hand. "I'm here for you. Don't feel you need to talk or entertain me. I could see your worry and didn't think you needed to be alone."

Mom told the nurse's station where they'd be and dragged him to the cafeteria for lunch. He tried to eat, but he only managed to eat about half of the chicken pie, the only thing he'd gotten.

His father came back at two o'clock. "No change," had been all Oliver had heard about Marie.

At two-thirty, Mom looked at the clock and then back at Oliver. "I'm so sorry, but I'm going to have to go. I need to be home when the kids get there, and I'll need to fix some supper. The girls aren't old enough to handle that."

He nodded his understanding but still hating to see her go. Now he would really feel alone.

She hugged him tightly before she left. "Now you call me the minute you know anything. Don't you forget. And remember that God is always with you."

"I won't forget." He just hoped he had something to call about soon.

A new nurse came in about seven. "I've talked with Dr. McCloud. He said that he will be by to see Marie first thing tomorrow morning when he does his rounds. If there hasn't been any progress, he'll order a C-section."

Oliver shivered as she left, and he didn't feel cold. By that time Marie would have been in labor for thirty hours. Surely that was way too long. If only he could be with her while they waited, it would help ease both their suffering.

At eight the next morning, the doctor came to see Oliver. He guessed he looked as haggard as he felt by the man's expression. He hadn't been able to eat or sleep, although he'd managed to keep some liquids down.

"I've ordered them to prep your wife for a C-section now." Dr. McCloud didn't appear at all concerned about the operation, but Oliver felt weak enough from the news to be glad he was seated.

"How is she?"

"Tired and worried but doing fine otherwise." He twisted his head to one side as if that would help him assess Oliver. "How would you like to see your wife before she goes back?"

Oliver almost jumped from his seat, finding new energy at the prospect.

"I'll tell them to hold up on the preparations and give you no more than five minutes with her. I think seeing you will help her relax." A devious grin spread across Dr. McCloud's face. "Unless you scare her with your red eyes, wrinkled brow, and disheveled hair. I suggest you go to the restroom, wash your face, and comb your hair. A nurse's aide will be waiting to take you back when you come out."

Oliver hurried to the restroom and then followed the lady to a cubicle close to the operating room. Marie looked every bit as worried and tired as the doctor said. He rushed to her side and picked up her hand.

"Oliver." She said his name as if she had been longing to see him.

"I'm so glad to finally get to see you." He kissed the back of her hand. "The waiting has been hard."

"For me, too." She looked at the light. "Do you think God is punishing me for the wrong I did? I don't want anything to happen to the baby because of my sins. I might deserve it, but it doesn't."

"No, honey. God doesn't work that way. And didn't you tell me you had asked for forgiveness? When God forgives, he remembers it no more."

She looked back at him, her eyes damp with unshed tears. "I wish you could stay with me. I don't want to have to do this alone."

"I wish I could have been with you this whole time, but they'll put you asleep for the Caesarean, and when you wake up, we'll have a son or daughter."

"I guess you want a boy. Daddy always did. That's why he never loved me much."

"I honestly don't care as long as it's healthy. And I think your daddy loves you. He just doesn't know how to show it." Oliver hoped that was true, anyway. He couldn't imagine someone not loving Marie.

"Has the labor been difficult?"

"No, just long. I feel some pressure, but the pains haven't been strong."

"It's time to go, Mr. Hartsell." The nurse looked ready to push him out.

"Already?" That had been the quickest five minutes of his life.

He kissed Marie lightly on the lips. "I love you," he whispered as he pulled back.

She squeezed his hand before she released it. The nurse had already pulled out a pan and razor as he walked through the curtain opening.

He found a pay phone and called home to let them know what was happening. Then, he went to the O.R. waiting room this time. A nurse promised to let him know when the operation had ended and Marie went to recovery. At that time, he would also know the gender of the baby. He didn't care about that as much as knowing Marie was all right. He bowed his head and prayed.

This waiting room had more people in it than the other one. He found a seat in the front corner that had fewer people around.

His parents walked in about nine and hugged him. "I brought Louise by to stay with you, but I need to go back home. I've got fences to repair from that last storm we had. I scotched them up temporarily, but they won't hold for long."

"Thank you." Oliver said it to both, but he looked at his mother. He needed her quiet strength right now.

"You look exhausted," Mom said when his dad had left.

He just nodded. No use denying it.

"Have you eaten?"

"I can't, but I've drunk some water, coffee, and chocolate milk."

Surprisingly she didn't try to force him to eat something. "Do you want me to get you some juice?"

"No, I don't think my stomach will take the acid right now. I'll wait until after I get to see Marie and the baby. After that, I should feel more like eating."

A nurse came to the room and walked up to him. The big smile on her face told him the news would be good. "Mr. Hartsell, you have a baby boy."

"And Marie?"

"She's doing fine. We got her prepped and into the operating room, and the anesthesiologist had just started to give her the anesthesia when she started having severe pain. We checked, and sure enough, she had started dilating more. We held up, and she delivered the baby in about thirty minutes." She almost laughed. "That's the first normal delivery I ever remember in the operating room."

"So, she didn't have to have the C-section?" His mother asked to clarify."

"No, and we're moving her up to a room in a few minutes. She'll be in room 205 if you want to meet her there, and you'll be able to view the baby through the maternity window as soon as he's cleaned up and settled."

"Praise God!" Mom hugged him again when the nurse left. "Let's go. I'll stay at the window while you check on Marie, and then I'll see her a little later. I like to look at the babies anyway."

Oliver had been waiting in the hall by room 205 about twenty minutes when they rolled Marie in. She looked even more exhausted than before.

We've given her some medication, and she's sleepy." The nurse said. "Let her get a nap if you can. Your son will demand to be fed before long, and we'll need to wake her then."

"Have you seen him?" She patted the edge of her bed for him to sit beside her.

He sat at an angle turned toward her head. "Not yet. I wanted to see you first. Mom is down there, though, and I'll go down soon."

She closed her eyes as if they were too heavy to hold open anymore. "I'm glad it's all over with, and I can't wait to take him home." She opened her eyes. "We never did decide on what to name a boy."

"I like all the names we talked about. You chose the one you like best."

She closed her eyes again, presumedly to think. "Let's call him Davy Andrew."

"Davy Andrew Hartsell. I like that." He smiled down at her.

She closed her eyes, and he heard her breathing ease. He got up to go see his son, because no matter how he was conceived, Davy Hartsell would always be his son.

"Isn't he just the cutest thing." Mom pointed to the largest baby in the nursery. Her face glowed with the anticipation of a new grandmother. "I can't wait for your father to see him."

I agree that he's special. We've named him Davy Andrew, by the way. But men don't take to babies the way women do."

"If you're talking about your dad, he'll take to this one because he's our first grandson."

Oliver nodded with his eyes firmly fixed on the baby. Nine pounds, two ounces, the card on the front of the clear plastic bassinet said. His blond hair and blue eyes reminded Oliver of Marie. He hoped the little fellow would turn out looking like his mama.

"His reddish skin will clear up soon." Mom followed his gaze. "But he's nicely filled out with hardly a wrinkle like most newborns."

"Isn't he breathing heavily?" Oliver asked.

"I noticed that, too, but I just figured it came from that long labor."

A nurse came and rolled Davy to the back. The urgency in her movements worried Oliver. He looked at his mom.

Her smiled faded, and her eyes squinted, causing furrows to crease her forehead. "I don't know what's happening, but I don't like the looks of this."

"Let's go back to Marie's room. If there's any news, someone will probably bring it there."

Marie still slept as they entered the room, but she roused as Oliver drew near to her bed. "Did you see Davy? Are they going to bring him for me to feed?"

"I saw him. He's a fine-looking boy." No sense in saying more and causing worry over little more than speculation at this point.

His mother stepped forward. "How are you feeling, honey?"

Marie gave a weak smile. "Still tired and sleepy, but I'm fine. I'm glad you came."

"I wouldn't miss seeing my handsome grandson as soon as possible."

About thirty minutes later, a young man walked into the room. "Mr. and Mrs. Hartsell? I'm Doctor Smith and work here at the hospital. Could we talk in private?" He looked at Oliver's mom.

She started to stand, but Marie interrupted. "This is my mother-in-law. She can stay."

The doctor looked to Oliver for confirmation and he nodded. He moved to take Marie's hand. This didn't look good.

"I've consulted with Dr. McCloud over the phone. Your son had developed some fluid on the brain. It happens to be on the section that controls the respiratory system, and he's having trouble breathing.

We're going to move him to an incubator to help him out."

"How bad is it?" Marie's grip tightened on Oliver's hand.

"It looks to be serious. At this point, I'd give him about a fifty-fifty chance, but babies are resilient, and that might change once we get him on oxygen."

"Will any of the rest of his brain be affected?" Oliver needed to know, although he hated to ask, especially in front of Marie."

"No, I don't think so. The fluid appears to be contained in that one area. If we can get his breathing back to normal, he should be fine." The tone of the doctor's voice suggested that might be a big "if."

Chapter Eighteen: The Hospital Stay

"Let's pray," Mom said as soon as the doctor left. They bowed their heads, and she said a beautiful prayer for Davy.

A nurse came in just as she finished. "The doctor wanted me to talk with you, Marie. I know you said you planned to breastfeed, but most mothers are bottle feeding these days. If you decide to breastfeed, we'll need to pump your milk until your son gets out of the incubator."

"I still want to breastfeed." Marie looked at Oliver, but that should be her decision. He just hoped his face wasn't as red as Davy's had been. However, she had originally decided to breastfeed to cut down on expenses, and he would feel bad if that was her only reason now. Sometimes he felt so inadequate.

"I'll check back with you, and we'll pump when you need it, but don't worry about your baby. He's been taken care of for now."

His father came to get Mom about two o'clock. Oliver went home for about two hours late that afternoon. but came back and stayed with Marie overnight. The lounge chair in the room felt fairly comfortable, and he dozed some when she did.

The Austins came in around eight, the next

morning. "We couldn't get a good look at the baby," Mrs. Austin said. "They had him in the back, behind the other babies, and his bassinet had a top to it, which the other ones didn't."

Oliver explained what had happened. He hadn't bothered to call them after his mother reported how nonchalant they'd acted when she'd called them.

Mr. Austin looked over a Marie. "You can't do anything right these days, can you?"

Tears welled in her eyes, and Oliver felt like punching the guy. "The situation has us worried enough as it is. If you're going to make cruel, heartless remarks, you need to leave."

Mrs. Austin gasped as if she didn't want to leave. Mr. Austin's eyes grew wide, but he didn't say another word. After nearly a minute of awkward silence, Mr. Austin turned to his wife. "I'll wait for you in the main lobby."

After her husband left, Mrs. Austin showed Marie more consideration, and Oliver could tell she appreciated her mother's visit. It would have been good if her mother could have been here for her before now.

Mrs. Austin didn't stay long. Oliver guessed she knew her husband wouldn't want her to, but the whole situation made him appreciate his family all the more.

Marie's blood pressure dropped that afternoon. Oliver knew she'd worried herself sick over Davy, but he would have thought that would make her blood pressure rise, not fall. She hadn't been eating much, so maybe that was part of the problem.

There had been talk she might get to go home tomorrow, although Davy would need to stay until he could come out of the incubator. Oliver guessed this new development would change that possibility. He swallowed back his disappointment. He just wanted to take his family home.

The preacher and his wife came by during evening visiting hours. "We got a glimpse of that little boy of yours in the nursery," Mrs. Barbee said. "He sure is a good-looking little fellow."

Marie perked up a little, but then her eyes quickly lost their luster. "If he'll just start breathing normally."

"He looks strong." Mrs. Barbee's face filled with sympathy. "I feel sure he'll be fine."

Oliver looked toward the ceiling and silently thanked God for positive people. Marie needed that. He needed that, too. Reverend Barbee said a prayer that sounded heartfelt, and they left.

Marie watched them walk from the room and then turned to Oliver. "Does the pastor's wife always visit at the hospital with him?"

He thought of when his father had had pneumonia so bad that Dr. McCloud didn't know if he would pull through or not. "I don't think so. Perhaps it's because she likes seeing the babies."

"I want to see my baby." Marie's voice trembled. "Do you think they would let us go to the nursery if you roll me down in a wheelchair?"

Oliver could well understand her need to see the baby. He had looked in on him a number of times, but Marie hadn't. "I'll go ask."

The nurse came in and checked her vitals. "Your blood pressure is back up to seventy-six over fifty-two. Not normal but better than earlier." She must have seen the desperate need in Marie's eyes. "If you will stay in the wheelchair until you get to the window, you lean on your husband when you stand to see, and you only stand for a couple of minutes, I don't think it will hurt. In fact, it might help. I just don't want you falling."

Marie leaned against the window more than she leaned on Oliver, but he kept an arm around her just in case. When he helped her sit back down, big tears rolled down her face. Maybe this hadn't been such a good idea after all.

"He's doing fine, Marie. Everyone says he's holding his own."

"And just what does that mean?" she muttered. "If anything happens to him, it will be because he has such a sorry Mama."

He bent down in front of her and took her hands. "That's just not true. You are a wonderful mother, and Davy is precious. We're going to be one of the happiest families around." He hoped. He prayed Davy would be okay, but he wouldn't let Marie see his own worry. He wished he could take the guilt she wanted to let burden her away. She had never been able to forgive herself.

She finally looked him in the eyes. "Do you really think he will be fine?"

"I do." He thought about adding that whatever happened they would face it together, but that sounded too fatalistic right now.

Some more people came to the window, so he rolled her back to the room and helped her to bed. The nurse almost followed them in to check on her and take her vitals again.

"Did you see how his little chest was almost jumping?" When she looked at him for an answer, he could see the fear in her eyes.

"The doctor said it might take a few days for the fluid to leave his brain. Have faith, darling."

He needed to take his own advice, for if Davy didn't make it, he didn't know how he could comfort Marie. *Oh, Lord, I pray that we don't have to face that.*

"Your son has shown remarkable improvement since I examined him yesterday," Dr. McCloud told them the next morning. "If he continues to improve, I think we can move him from the incubator tomorrow." He chuckled. "Those incubators were made for preemies, not nine-pound, two-ounce boys. Did you see how he nearly filled up that incubator?"

Marie actually smiled at the doctor's gentle teasing, and Oliver smiled at her. Now, maybe she would quit worrying so much. *Thank You, Lord.*

Her blood pressure had come up to within the normal range, and she ate more of her breakfast than usual.

"I don't like their dry biscuits, and I don't feel like eating the bacon or drinking the orange juice this morning. You eat them." She pushed her tray table toward him.

She had eaten all her eggs and grits and drunk her milk. He hadn't seen her eat that much here.

"Are you sure?" he asked.

She nodded. "There's no sense in letting it go to waste."

She sounded so much like his mother, he almost laughed. It felt good because he hadn't felt like laughing much lately either.

Marie freshened up in the bathroom and wanted to walk down to the nursery. It will be better for me to move around some than to lay in that bed all the time," she assured him.

They both felt better as they watched Davy sleeping peacefully. His breathing looked normal, and his chest no longer rose and fell as if he labored hard.

Oliver enjoyed the day he spent with Marie

without worry eating at them. He tried not to think of how much work he had missed, and how that would affect his pay.

Mr. Austin would likely complain about him not fulfilling his obligations to work for the car, too, but the man better not renege on their deal. Oliver would go by there as soon as he got Marie home and settled. Now that Davy had improved, that shouldn't be long.

"I want you to go home and get some sleep," Marie told him that evening. "I know that chair can't be comfortable."

"Being with you makes me more comfortable. That house would seem awfully empty and lonely without you."

If it didn't get dark so early now, he might have gone to work on her father's farm, but if he went home to sleep, he didn't think he'd get much for wanting to be with Marie.

"I could release you this morning," Dr. McCloud told Marie the next morning, "but with you breastfeeding, I think it's better to keep you. "Your son is out of the incubator and doing fine, but I want to keep him one more day to be sure. If all goes well, you can take him home tomorrow morning. In the meantime, the nurse will bring him to you and help you get him to nursing."

The look on Marie's face showed a mixture of joyous excitement and trepidation. Oliver knew all of this was new to her, too.

"We didn't get to celebrate Valentine's Day with you in the hospital," he said after the doctor left. "Maybe we can do something special tomorrow or soon if you feel up to it. Mama would be thrilled to keep Davy for us to go out, or I could go get us something and bring home if you didn't want to do that."

"Just getting to go home seems special." Had she started to blush? "And Davy is our Valentine's gift. You don't need to do anything special, but we'll talk about it again when we get home if you want to."

Oliver had bought her a card, but he'd planned to get her something else, too. Maybe he could still do that.

"I appreciate you staying here with me all this time," Marie told Oliver while they waited for the wheelchair to come. She looked down at Davy, wrapped snuggly in blankets. She couldn't get enough of seeing him.

"There's nowhere else I wanted to be." Oliver

took a step closer to the chair, so he could get a better look, too. "I've been praying I'll be the best husband and father possible."

"You already have a good start with that." Marie had no problem saying that to Oliver. However, she couldn't say that she'd be the best mother or wife. She felt Oliver had treated her better than she'd treated him.

However, he had only promised to give her until the baby came before they started sharing the same bedroom, and she wondered when he would expect that, now that the baby had come. Knowing Oliver, he would give her several days to recover first.

She realized she didn't panic at the thought of sharing a bed with him the way she had at first. However, she still didn't want it and didn't look forward to it. Yet, a large part of her wanted Oliver to be happy. He was such a good man and had treated her so well. She knew he would also treat Davy well, and her son couldn't ask for a better father.

The biggest problem still resided in the fact that he wasn't Derrick. She almost scoffed out loud. Since Derrick had refused to marry her, it was better Oliver wasn't like him.

The nurse's aide pushed the wheelchair into the room. Oliver held Davy while the aide helped Marie into the wheelchair, although she didn't really need any help. She might move a little more slowly due to the small amount of soreness that remained, but she could move around fine.

Oliver handed Davy back to her, picked up the things they had packed, and hurried toward the parking lot to get the car and bring it around for her. She looked around as they left, glad to be leaving this place.

Davy began to fret when they got outside, but once they were in the car and began to move, he fell back asleep. Her spirits picked up from getting out of the hospital. That small, drab room could be depressing.

Marie couldn't wait to get home and to get to hold her baby whenever she wanted. That hospital stay had been too long, and having Davy isolated in the incubator made it even more difficult.

She looked at Oliver wondering what the future held. She might never love him like she did Derrick, but she thought she could be content in their marriage. Maybe that would be enough.

Chapter Nineteen: The Meeting

When they got home, they found the house warm with a fire going in the woodstove. Oliver moved the bassinet into the living room for now.

"Dad or one of the boys must have lit the fire for us." Oliver added another stick of firewood to the stove.

"That was thoughtful." Marie had never expected such generosity as the Hartsells showed. She hadn't grown up with it

"I want to help you with Davy," Oliver held him while she fixed them some sandwiches for lunch. "Let me keep him in my bedroom at least every other night for now. When he just needs his diaper changed, I can take care of it. When he needs to be fed, I'll bring him to you or use a bottle if you pump some. That way, you won't have to get up."

She couldn't believe his offer, but she felt sure she'd appreciate his help as the nights of getting little sleep mounted up. "I'll take him tonight, then, and you can see to him tomorrow night."

"Do you think Davy will be warm enough at night if we take him to a bedroom with us?" Oliver looked down at the baby as he spoke.

"I think so if we leave the door open and keep the fire going through the night."

"I might need to see about getting an electric heater for him. I'd want to get a new one and not a used one, however, because they've been known to start fires."

"That's something to consider. Maybe we could just get one to use when the temperature dips low anyway." Oliver had always been caring and considerate, but moments like this still surprised her.

"Let's plan a special day in lieu of the Valentine's Day we missed." Oliver looked across the table at breakfast. "We'll make it on February the twenty-eight. That will be exactly two weeks after Valentine's Day, and you should be about fully recovered by then."

She swallowed hard to get her bite of cereal down. Oliver had insisted they eat something simple she didn't have to cook. Did he hint that this would be a good time to consummate their marriage?

She looked him in the eyes but couldn't tell if he had an ulterior motive. "What did you have in mind?"

"That depends on what you'd prefer. Would you like to leave Davy with Mom and go out to eat?"

"Could we do something here instead. Davy is usually good, but you could take him to your mom's if he becomes too fussy."

He nodded. "I'll get two steaks then. I want this

to be special."

"It might be too cold to grill them outside." They had a rusty old grill that had been left by some tenant.

"I'll be fine with a coat, and the grill will keep me warm enough for no longer than it will take."

"Then I'll fix us baked potatoes, salad, and maybe a dessert."

He reached over and put his hand over hers. He did that a lot. "You just take care of the potatoes and salad. I don't want you doing too much. I'll pick us up a dessert."

"Okay, if that's what you want, but a store-bought dessert won't be as good as homemade."

"I'll see what I can do about that." His sly grin gave her pause, but she let it drop.

It didn't take long for things to fall into a new routine. Oliver resumed work, and Marie had Davy all to herself during most days. She soon became extra thankful for Oliver's help during the night. Yet, she knew he would soon expect to move into the main bedroom with her, and the night of their special meal seemed to be the most logical time. In a strange way, she dreaded that night but also felt curious about it. Could it be that she liked him more than she thought?

A letter came for her that had no return address, and her address had been typed instead of handwritten.

Yet, the postmark said it had been mailed from Albemarle.

The mail usually came midmorning while Oliver was at the hardware. She poured herself the last cup of coffee and sat down to open it.

My darling Marie,

Meet me at the entrance to Morrow Mountain this Friday morning, March 24, at 10:00. We'll talk then.

Love forever,
Derrick

Her hand trembled as she finished the note. This Friday. Just a few days away. What could he want? Perhaps he wanted to see Davy, but he didn't say to bring the baby.

Should she even go? Meeting him without it being prearranged felt bad enough, but answering his summons felt much worse. She would have to give this some thought.

Oliver watched her closely that afternoon. "You seem preoccupied. Is anything wrong? If you need a break, take Davy to Mom's for the morning. As long as you pick him up by the time school lets out, it should be fine. Of course, the girls would love to get their hands on him, too, if you run late, but you might not want that."

"I'm fine. Nothing out of the ordinary for a new mother."

Impulsively, she bent over and kissed his cheek, suddenly taken with his kindness and caring. He pulled her down on his lap and thoroughly kissed her lips. She felt herself turn warm in his arms, like melted butter.

Davy cried, and she gathered her strength to stand. "I'll see what he needs. He's probably hungry." She hoped her voice hadn't trembled.

What would have happened if Davy hadn't cried out? Oliver had begun to affect her much more than she ever suspected he might.

Friday morning came, and Marie still had no idea if she would meet Derrick or not. Her reaction to Oliver confused her. She didn't know if her affections were moving from Derrick to Oliver or if that had just been a moment of weakness that wouldn't be repeated. Perhaps she had turned into a tramp as her father said.

Maybe seeing Derrick would at least give her some clarity. She would know when she saw him if she still loved him or if she had begun to care more for Oliver.

When Oliver left for work, she took her time getting Davy and herself ready. She debated over whether or not to take the baby to her mother-in-law's as Oliver had once suggested or take him with her. In the end, she decided to take him. Derrick had a right to see his son. She bundled Oliver up and put him in a padded box in the front seat, so he would be easier to manage alone in the car.

Her heart pounded harder the closer she got to the entrance of the state park. Something about coming here had rattled her nerves, but she hoped she would calm down once she met up with Derrick.

She looked over at Davy as she pulled up toward the gate and parked in a parking spot. He looked so cute he would have to soften Derrick's heart. His complexion had cleared, and he'd begun to fill out. His blue eyes looked right at her. She would let Derrick see his son no matter what happened.

"Hey, baby." Derrick opened her car door and leaned in to give her a kiss, but she turned her head so that it landed on her cheek. "Come on, let's go down a trail where we can be alone." He nodded toward the forest.

"I've got the baby with me, and I don't want to keep him out in the cold for too long. I thought you might want to see your son."

Derrick grimaced. "I'd rather have you alone without any encumbrances but come on to my car."

She took Davy out of his makeshift bed and made sure he was well covered. She could hold him in her lap better without the box, and Derrick's Corvette had no other place to set it.

When they got inside Derrick turned to her. "It's so good to see you. After what you said in Oakboro the last time, I wasn't sure you would come."

"I was curious to see what you wanted."

"I want you." The look he gave Marie made her glad the console sat between them.

She unwrapped Davy and angled him, so Derrick could get a good view. "Isn't he adorable?"

He shrugged. "Baby's look all the same to me. At least, you had a boy. The others have all had girls."

His bright red face let Marie know he hadn't meant to say that. "How many others?"

"What do you mean?"

"How many other women have there been?"

He shrugged again. "They're in the past. I only want you now?"

"How many baby girls have you fathered, Derrick?"

"You're not going to let this drop, are you?"

"No. I think I have a right to know, and my imagination will likely make it worse than it really is."

"Three, I guess."

Marie stiffened. Or maybe reality would be worse than she had imagined. By his tone of voice, three that he knew of. Who was this man? Not the man she thought she loved.

She had made up her mind to get out of his car and go back home when he put it in gear and started driving. "Let's go to the top. We need to talk,"

He said nothing as the Corvette hung the curves with ease. He must know enough to give her some time. She'd give him a chance to say what he wanted to say, and then she would leave. For good. This would be her last and final goodbye.

The car ride put Davy back to sleep. He didn't wake up when Derrick parked in front of the rock wall.

"Can you lay him down and come out with me," Derrick whispered.

She nodded, and Derrick closed his door silently without latching it before hurrying around to open her door. She eased out and lay Davy gently in the bucket seat. Derrick closed her door like he had his.

"We'll need to stay where the car is in sight," she told him, and he nodded.

He took her hand and led her just a few feet to a place where they could see Badin Lake as a small spot in the distance. "I need you, Marie. I'm having a hard time doing without you. I don't think I could stand it if you reject me."

She looked at him carefully, thinking he was probably just feeding her a line, but he looked sincere. Yet, his touch hadn't produced the tingles it had in the past.

"But you don't want Davy." She didn't ask it as a question because she knew the answer.

"Can't you see? He'd just get in the way. I want all your attention, and I want to give you all of mine. We deserve some time alone. That's what I crave."

"And what am I supposed to do with Davy?" She had no intention of doing anything with her son, but she wanted to hear what he would say.

"I bet Oliver would take the kid. He's a sucker like that. If not, you could always put him up for adoption."

She tried not to speak through clenched teeth. "And what am I supposed to do – leave Oliver?

"That would be great, and it's what I'm hoping for, but until you can work it out, we could meet somewhere while Oliver's at work. Your place might not work best, but we could go to a motel if you didn't want to just stay in the car. You should be able to find someone to keep the kid for a couple of hours. Right?"

She heard what sounded like a group of children chattering in the distance, but she didn't look to see. It took all her effort to control her anger with Derrick and come to terms with what a jerk he had turned out to be.

"It's always been all about you, hasn't it? What you want, what you need, fulfilling your desires,

"No, baby. That's not true. I want you to be happy, too. I know what makes you happy, now, don't

I?"

"Just seeing you used to make me happy," she admitted.

"Ah-h, don't put that in the past tense. I can still make you happy. I promise." He held his arms open. "Come here."

She hesitated, but then stepped into his arms. She knew he planned to kiss her, and she wanted to see if his kisses affected her the way they used to. Besides, this would definitely be a goodbye kiss. She had no intention of seeing him again.

If she didn't miss her guess, he'd likely been seeing someone else since he found out she was pregnant. Derrick would not be without a woman for long, and she would never be able to trust him. Oh, how she wished she had seen this earlier, but he did a good job of saying what a girl wanted to hear.

When she didn't respond to his kiss as passionately as before, he doubled the intensity. Regrettably, his kiss still pulled at her, but not as much as it once did.

She heard the roar of a large engine and pulled back in time to see the back of a blue and white activity bus. Great. Now they had put on a show for a group of school kids.

Derrick followed her gaze and frowned. "What are those kids doing on a field trip here in the winter?"

"They probably had a program at the museum

and just came up here to see the view.

"Yeah, well they must have used the bathrooms here, too, from the sounds they were making." He shrugged. "But it really doesn't make any difference. I don't want to talk about kids. When can you see me again? What about Monday?"

"Never." She started walking toward the car.

He ran toward her and grabbed her arm. "You don't mean that."

"Oh, but I do. Just take me back to my car."

"And what if I refuse?" He looked way too smug.

"Then I guess Davy and I will start walking. At least, it's downhill, and someone will probably come along to pick us up. I need to get to the car where it's private and feed Davy."

"You're breastfeeding him?" He smirked. "I'd like to see that."

Marie grew so angry tears formed in her eyes. Jerk didn't even begin to describe him. He had turned out to be such a disappointment.

Chapter Twenty: The Mistake

Derrick dropped her back at her car. "You'll change your mind. You're just having a bad day, but you want me about as much as I want you. I'll give you some time to come to your senses before I contact you again."

"Don't bother." She held onto Davy and got out of the car before Derrick could come around.

She put Davy in his improvised bed. He watched her intently but did fuss. Maybe she could make it home before he started crying for his milk. She could always pull over in a secluded spot if she needed to.

When Oliver came home that afternoon, she nearly ran from her bedroom and met him at the table as he sat his things down. "What's up?"

She wanted to run into his arms where she knew she'd find comfort, but she felt too awkward since she'd never done that before. "I'm just glad you're home."

He stared into her eyes and then pulled her into his arms. It was almost uncanny how he often instinctively knew what she needed. "I am, too. Especially with a welcome like this."

He smoothed some of her hair back away from

her face. "Have you had a hard day?"

"Yes. Harder than usual, anyway."

"Something smells good." He looked over at the stove. "And it's making me hungry."

"I have a beef stew ready. Come on. Let's eat." Her hand slid down his arm to take his hand and lead him to the table.

Saturday morning, Marie and Oliver went to town and purchased a few of the things they needed but had been unable to buy. The inheritance check had come from the lawyer, but the largest portion would go to pay the hospital bill.

Davy became fussy about midday and became worse as the afternoon wore on. By suppertime, Marie could tell he had a fever, and she sent Oliver to the store to get him some infant pain reliever.

It didn't help much, and they took turns walking the floor with him or rocking him. He wouldn't settle down.

"We'll just postpone our Valentine's supper until next Saturday," Oliver told her. "I can put the steaks in the freezer."

She nodded feeling a strange sense of disappointment. "You might wait and see how he's doing tomorrow. We might get to have it then. If he's better, we could leave him with your mother after church." She looked down at Davy. If he wasn't better, she wouldn't be going to church or the Hartsells.

All three of them got little sleep that night. They napped a little when Davy dozed off, but his naps were short, and so were theirs. Oliver tried to take care of Davy some, so she could sleep, but sleep didn't come easily with the baby crying.

Davy quietened down and fell into a peaceful slumber about four o'clock. He woke them up again at eight, but she could detect no fever, he appeared comfortable, and he took his milk for breakfast like usual.

After he had finished, Marie found Oliver in the kitchen. "Davy seems to be well this morning. Do you think we can go to church?"

Oliver looked at Davy. "I'd like to. We can always bring him back home if his temperature comes back. What do you think was wrong?"

She shook her head. "I have no idea. Perhaps it was a short-lived virus or something. He's too young to be cutting teeth."

"Well, he seems to be doing much better, and that's the main thing."

Davy made it through church without any problems, so they went to the Hartsell home for Sunday dinner, like usual. Marie always enjoyed visiting there.

"How did your field trip go, Friday?" Oliver

asked Annie, his youngest sister, as they finished eating.

"It was fun." She looked at Marie as if suddenly remembering something. "Who was that you were kissing at Morrow Mountain, Marie?"

The room grew deathly silent, and Marie felt her entire body freeze into a block of ice.

Mrs. Hartsell's eyes skittered from Marie to Oliver to Annie. "I'm sure you were just mistaken, honey. You must have seen someone who looked like Marie."

The girl huffed as if she'd had experience with not being believed. "I did, too, see Marie. Her car was even parked down next to the gate when the bus left. It would be hard to mistake that pink car."

Marie couldn't think of a thing to say. She looked at Oliver and he stared at her with stone-hard eyes. He stood. "I guess we need to be going. Since Davy was sickly last night, I don't want to keep him out too long."

No one protested, and Marie stood to follow Oliver out. She felt so drained she barely had the strength to move, and the chicken 'n dumplings she had eaten soured in her stomach.

"You come to see me if you need to talk," Mrs. Hartsell said as Marie left the kitchen, but the woman didn't get up from her seat.

Oliver didn't say a word on the drive home, and

Marie didn't either. She guessed he didn't want to have such an important conversation while driving.

She tried to think through what she would say, but she knew she wouldn't lie. She would just explain how the meeting had gone and what a jerk Derrick had been, and hopefully, Oliver would understand.

She stole another glance at him. His face could have been one of the faces chiseled on Mount Rushmore. *Oh, Lord, let him be understanding.* But it didn't look promising.

When they got home, she went to the bedroom to put Davy in his bassinet. She would have liked to close the door, throw herself on her bed, and sob. But that would only postpone the inevitable. No, better to get this over with. With another brief prayer, she went to try to placate her husband.

She found him pacing the floor in the kitchen. Seeking reprieve, if only for a moment, she sat down on the loveseat. He walked to her with deliberate steps.

"It was Derrick, wasn't it?" It sounded more like a proclamation than a question.

What could she say? "Yes, I agreed to meet him to see what he wanted and to let him see Davy."

He gave her such an incredulous look she almost doubted herself. "And you kissed him?"

"It was a goodbye kiss."

He scoffed. "And was this the first time you've seen him?"

She couldn't look at him. "No, he unexpectedly came here once uninvited, and I ran into him once in Oakboro."

"He came here? To our house?" She nodded, searching for something to say that would make sense and she hadn't already said, but he continued. "And when you ran into him in Oakboro, what did you do?"

She swallowed, trying to clear a dry scratchy throat. "We went to his car to talk for a few minutes."

"You expect me to believe you've met with him three times, and all you've ever done was talk."

"It is…."

He put up his hand to stop her. "Yeah, and Davy is proof that all you've ever done with Derrick is talk."

That was the closest thing to being cruel to her as Oliver had ever come. She recognized it as an attempt to strike back from the deep hurt her actions had inflicted on him, but that didn't take away the sting of his words. "I am sorry…."

The hand came up again. "I don't want to hear it. Not another word." The pain in his face brought tears to her eyes. "What a fool I've been, but no more. You've gone behind my back to see another man, the man who fathered your child, and, in my book, that's cheating on me. I can't bear another word right now." With that, he turned and left.

When she didn't hear the truck start up, she

assumed he went to the shed where he had his workshop. She had wanted to say so much that she hadn't been able to tell him. Maybe if she gave him time to calm down, he would listen to her explanations.

She went to her room, buried her head in her pillow, and cried, trying to stay quiet enough not to wake Davy. Without a doubt, she'd just made one of the biggest mistakes of her life when she'd gone to meet Derrick on Morrow Mountain.

After a length of time, she didn't know how long, Davy awoke hungry. She pulled herself together enough to feed him, but he didn't nurse as well as usual. He likely could sense her agitation.

Oliver didn't come in for supper, and Marie didn't feel like eating either. They wouldn't have their romantic Valentine's supper. She had seen the candles Oliver had bought and knew what they were for.

When Davy went back to sleep, she fell on her knees, needing some kind of help and comfort. She didn't even know what to pray for, but she just let her heart cry out. Her heart bled that she had wounded Oliver so deeply. He had been wonderful to her, the best husband possible under the circumstances, and she had betrayed him. He couldn't hate her any more than she hated herself. What had she been thinking! What was she going to do?

What a fool he'd been. Oliver told himself for the hundredth time. Marie had said from the first that she'd never love him, but he wouldn't listen to her. He truly thought God had blessed their union, but he must have been mistaken. He surely believed what she'd tried to tell him now.

Still, that she would see Derrick behind his back stunned him and shocked him to his core. And it had happened more than once. He had been more naïve than he'd ever considered. He had believed in Marie, trusted her. Well, no more, and if he couldn't trust her, he couldn't believe anything she said. Common sense said that she had slept with Derrick on at least one of those times, and she had definitely been kissing him.

He felt dead inside now, but, at the same time, he had never hurt so much. *God help me! Take away some of this pain; I can't bear it. Show me what to do; I am adrift in a sea of despair. Have mercy on me, I pray.*

What God hath joined together, let no man put asunder. Where had that come from? It sounded like a Bible verse, but it wasn't one he had ever memorized. How did it get in his head? Was God telling him to honor his marriage vows.

Did he even want to divorce Marie? He had never thought of such a thing before. He would give her a divorce if she asked for one, he decided, but he wouldn't initiate one himself. Those wedding vows were sacred.

What then? Live in a loveless marriage the rest of his life? He couldn't imagine the misery. He would never have biological children of his own, because he wouldn't be intimate with Marie if she didn't love him and want him for a husband. That would be too much like prostituting. He couldn't stand the thoughts of her wishing he were Derrick while he made love to her.

"A wife of noble character is her husband's crown, but a disgraceful wife is like decay in his bones," Oliver quoted back the verse from Proverbs he remembered from his nightly Bible study last week. It had stuck with him because it had hit him as odd but also had given him a clear mental picture.

He who finds a wife finds what is good and receives favor from the Lord.

Oliver snorted. "God, You couldn't be saying what Marie has done is good. I doubt that you even wanted me to marry her. I probably jumped ahead of You, and You had something or someone else planned for me."

Then, he remembered the story of Hosea and Gomer. God had told the prophet to marry the prostitute, and she bore him three children, but she had also left him for another man. He had found her and bought her back from the man, paying half the price of a slave. Although Oliver knew, God was showing how Israel had deserted Him for other gods, he had never fully understood that story. Surely God hadn't wanted him to marry Marie, considering what had happened now.

For my thoughts are not your thoughts, neither are your ways my ways.

Could these thoughts really be coming from God? They were definitely coming from the Bible. Was he standing here arguing with God? If so, he'd surely lose.

He wished he knew for certain exactly what God wanted him to do, but God usually led one step at a time and not by revealing the whole plan.

All he knew to do was wait and see where God led. For now, he would do nothing about Marie, but he had lost all hope that they would ever be happy. He couldn't pretend to be content when he had never been so miserable. If she wanted to leave him, he wouldn't try to stop her.

He fell on his knees on the cold, hard boards that made up the floor in the shed and prayed. He needed God's direction more than ever before. He needed God.

Tears washed his face as he poured out his

bleeding heart. He had no idea how long he prayed, but when he finished, he felt a little more at peace, even though the deep, cutting ache hadn't left.

He went back to the house trying to be as quiet as he could, so he wouldn't wake either Marie or Davy. It was her night to tend the baby, but he doubted if he would get much sleep anyway. Maybe he would spend the night reading his Bible and praying. At least tomorrow would be a workday, and he wouldn't have to stay around the house all day. He didn't even want to look at Marie.

Chapter Twenty-One: Pain

Monday turned out to be the longest day of Marie's life. She methodically went about sewing and doing household chores, but she hurt. Every fiber in her ached to the very core. She felt her own pain, but even more, she ached for the pain she'd caused Oliver, and that pain never quit slicing at her.

Only Davy brought her any comfort at all, but even cuddling him close or nursing him brought tears to her eyes. He might be all she had left.

When Oliver didn't come home at his regular time, she guessed he needed to work a little late. It hadn't occurred often, but it had happened. When the clock neared seven, she quit trying to keep the food hot for him.

"Where have you been?" Marie didn't mean to confront him the moment he walked in the front door. "It's nine o'clock at night, and I've been worried."

He didn't meet her eyes. "I didn't think you'd care, and I'm sure you knew I wasn't with another woman. I helped Dad split some wood. After all, he's helped us out with firewood."

"Of course, I care. Oliver, I didn't mean to hurt you."

"Enough!" He glared at her. "I don't want to hear anything about what you did Friday. I don't want to think about it."

Very well, she'd stay in the present then. "You could have stopped by and let me know so I wouldn't have tried to keep supper warm for you so long. It's cold now, but I'll reheat it."

"Don't bother. I'm not hungry. In fact, don't even fix supper for me from here on out. I'm going to be helping Dad and the boys more, and I'm going to try to finish up the repairs I promised to do for your father. If I get hungry, I'll grab something from Mom."

Marie's empty stomach started to knot. She could tell Oliver didn't want to be around her. And why did he want to finish the work for Daddy as soon as he could? Did he plan on leaving her?

When they started to their bedrooms, Oliver rolled Davy and his bassinet into his room. Marie followed.

"I didn't expect you'd want to keep him over the night anymore?" Would she ever understand this man?

He stopped abruptly and turned to her so that she almost ran into him. "Why would you think that? None of this is Davy's fault. In fact, he's the most innocent one in the whole sordid story."

She stood there watching Oliver push the bassinet into his room and close the door. And she could be judged the guiltiest one of all, certainly more guilty than Davy or Oliver.

The only choice she saw was to take it all to God. She prayed as she'd never prayed before – for Oliver and for herself. She read her Bible and began to see with clarity what the remarkable gift of grace was all about. It was not what she did, not her sins, but what Jesus had sacrificed and who He was. She could actually trade all her sinfulness for His righteousness. She could be forgiven and be holy in Him. It was hard to believe, but she did believe. For the first time in her life, she felt free and close to her Lord.

Tuesday morning, Marie couldn't stand it anymore. The walls fell as if they kept her from breathing. She needed someone to talk to and could think of no one. She wouldn't even consider her parents. Mary Jane and her former friends gossiped too much to share such private information, and she wouldn't want to tell them everything anyway. The preacher might be an option, but she really didn't know him well enough, and she'd prefer to talk to a woman.

Mrs. Hartsell might work out, but could she confide all of this to Oliver's mother? Wouldn't she take her son's side and be as upset with Marie as Oliver?

But she remembered what Mrs. Hartsell had told her after Annie had unknowingly thrown the venomous snake out into the room. "You come to see me if you need to talk."

Marie gathered Davy and drove to her mother-in-law's house about nine o'clock. Hopefully, she and Mrs. Hartsell would have time to talk before she needed to start cooking lunch.

Marie couldn't tell the story without tears flowing down her cheeks, but thankfully, she didn't have to stop due to sobs, and her voice only trembled at the roughest spots. Mrs. Hartsell didn't stop to interrupt her but sat quietly holding Davy. Yet, Marie didn't feel harsh judgment.

"I can tell you know you made a mistake in seeing Derrick and that you also know you've hurt Oliver deeply, so I won't say those things. What do you really want, Marie? Had you rather be with Oliver, with Derrick, or on your own?"

She hadn't expected that question, and she answered without thinking. "Oliver. I want my kind, caring, generous husband back."

Mrs. Hartsell's face brightened. "I was hoping you'd think that.

"He's just so hard and bitter and uncaring now. I don't know what to do. He won't let me explain anything, and we're both miserable. He's made it clear he doesn't want to see me or hear me."

"I understand that it's a hard situation, but Oliver's hurting too much right now to be reasonable. Give him time. My son feels deeply, loves deeply, and hurts deeply. Give him time for the knife to be removed from his heart. He'll still be hurting, but the pain won't be quite so sharp. Then, you should be able to get him to listen."

"Do you think he can ever forgive me?"

"Oh, I'm pretty sure he'll eventually forgive you, but getting back to trusting you may be a whole different problem. Once he's ready to talk, it wouldn't surprise me if he doesn't come to me or his dad, and it's usually me. Maybe I can soften the way for you to talk to him. I'll try, but I'll need to wait and pick my time. If I do it too early, it could hurt the situation more than help it."

"Thank you. Thank you for listening and being so understanding. Just talking to you has helped. Keeping all this bottled inside has about suffocated me."

"I imagine Oliver feels much the same way, only worse. I'll see if I can't get him alone sometime soon. Don't lose hope, Marie, but you're going to have to find a lot of patience. Healing is not going to come quickly for you two."

Marie nodded. She had been afraid of that, and she didn't mind waiting if there would be a good outcome. However, if Oliver would never again look at her with loving eyes, never again give her that special smile of his, or never treat her as if he'd found a special treasure in her, why endure all his contempt. It would be better to get out of the cold, dark prison she found herself in.

But then, where would she go? Her father would never take her back. Her only option would be to turn to Derrick, but she might have to give up Davy before Derrick would accept her. She couldn't bear the thought of that.

Maybe Oliver would move out and let her stay in the little house. She saw two problems with that, however. If he moved back in with his parents, she would still be much too close to him for comfort. And her daddy might not let her stay here if Oliver and she separated, and he still owned the house.

Even if he did let her stay, how would she work, pay for daycare, and make ends meet? How complicated life had gotten. She remembered a time when she thought if she could just finish school, things would get much simpler. How stupid and naïve of her.

As the days passed, Oliver gradually became less tense and rigid, but he still stayed in his workshop or at his parents' house much of the time. When he came in the house, he never made another cutting comment, but he couldn't be called the least bit friendly either. He remained aloof and withdrawn, but he willingly made needed statements and comments without a tone of contempt. If she had to name it, Marie would call his attitude one of reserved tolerance.

She tried to be pleasant and helpful, hoping her

approach would coax him to be more open to forgiving her, but she saw no progress there. How ironic that where Oliver had once tried to woo her, in a way, their roles had now reversed. Like his mother had said, she needed all the patience she could find.

By the looks she gave him, Oliver could tell his mother wanted to talk with him. Mom had always been perceptive, especially when it came to her family, and he knew she saw things had become strained between him and Marie. Besides, she had heard Annie's shocking statement, too. However, he didn't feel like talking about it yet. He wouldn't be able to until he could do so without causing the pain to intensify beyond endurance.

Strangely enough, Marie had grown gentler and kinder with him than ever. She tried to make things easier for him, but she couldn't. Her very presence made his stomach knot and the serrated knife she had embedded start sawing at his heart again.

He had no joy nor hope. He merely tried to make it one more day by enduring moment by moment. He spent much of his time alone in prayer to keep his mind off places that brought more pain. Little by little, God had brought some ease, but never enough. He would try to examine what God wanted him to do as soon as he got to the place where he could consider alternatives and make decisions, but he hadn't gotten there yet.

But the Lord held and carried him when he couldn't manage himself. He could feel His presence, and it kept him from thinking about suicide. He would live without Marie if need be, but he just had to get through this intense pain of where his whole world had turned upside down and shattered in thousands of sharp, dangerous shards. Never in his wildest imagination would he have thought she would sneak behind his back to be with Derrick. He had completely trusted her. He had been a total moron.

Two weeks later, Oliver went inside his parent's house to wash up before going home. He had been helping his brothers clean and straighten the barn, and it showed. He stood for a moment when he realized he still thought of the little house more as his home than here. Truth be told, however, he had no longer had a home. He felt adrift, uncomfortable everywhere.

"You're here late." His mother looked at the kitchen clock. "You should have been home hours ago."

He shrugged. "It's not so easy there. In fact, it's

- 261 -

not easy anywhere, but working with those crazy brothers of mine helps take my mind off the heartache for brief moments."

"Care to explain that." She sat down at the kitchen table as if she had all day to listen.

"Where're the girls?"

"They had homework, so I told them I could handle supper tonight."

"You know about Marie meeting Derrick on Morrow Mountain."

She nodded but said nothing, waiting for him to continue. Her calmness soothed him and made it easier to talk.

"Well, that wasn't the first time they'd met." He found the whole story pouring out like a ruptured dam, not only what had happened but also his feelings. When he choked up and had to take a moment before he could continue, his mother would put her hand over his as if some of her strength could be transferred to him. And maybe it could because he always managed to swallow and continue on. "What am I do?" he asked when he'd finished. "I don't know what to do."

She squeezed his hand more tightly. "What do you want to happen?"

"I want the woman I thought I married back, but that's not who Marie is. I've seen what I wanted to see and married the woman I thought she was, not the one she really is."

Mom sat back, releasing his hand. "Are you sure about that? Marie knows she made a terrible mistake. We all make mistakes, Oliver. You're supposed to be able to forgive."

He thought. "I might be able to forgive, but I don't know if I can accept her as my wife after she's betrayed me like this."

"Those wedding vows you spoke said for better or for worse." Mom's voice remained soft and gentle, but the words still smarted. He didn't want to be reminded of wedding vows.

"Marie broke those vows when she kissed Derrick and whatever else they did."

Mom touched his arm, forcing him to look at her. "Do you really think she did more than kiss him with Davy with her in a Corvette? I know kissing was bad enough and certainly wrong, but I don't think it's gone any farther than that."

"I don't know what to think. He came by the house before Davy was born. For all I know, they could have gone into the bedroom."

"She could have, but I don't think she did. Has there ever been a time that you knew without a doubt that Marie lied to you? Have you ever caught her in a lie?"

He had to shake his head. "But that doesn't mean she hasn't."

"It seems to me if she were going to lie, she

- 263 -

would have lied about seeing Derrick. She didn't have to tell you about the other two times, now did she? Marie came to talk to me on the Tuesday after Annie shared the news of what she'd seen."

Oliver's head jerked up and he stared at his mother. "I hadn't expected that. How much did she tell you?"

"Pretty much everything. She's hurting, too, you know, but she's hurting for you more than anything else. Knowing how disappointed you are in her and knowing that she's caused you so much pain is tearing her up inside."

He almost said that she'd brought all that on herself, but the thought died before he released it to words. Did that mean Marie did care for him? If she really cared for him, surely, she wouldn't have done what she had.

"I asked her what she wanted, just like I asked you. I also asked her if she'd rather be with you, Derrick, or on her own. Do you know what she said?"

"No, but it wouldn't have been with me."

"That's where you're wrong, because that's exactly what she said. And she answered the question about what she wanted by saying she wanted her kind, caring, generous husband back."

He couldn't believe it. "Are you sure?"

"That's exactly what she said."

"She likely just said it because you're my

mother, and it's what you wanted to hear. I can't believe she really feels that way."

"You're determined to see the worst in her, aren't you? That's a reaction to the hurt, Oliver, but it will bury both of you in a ton of misery if you don't stop."

She must have seen the look on his face, because she added. "I don't expect you to let it all go and forget it ever happened right now. I know that's impossible. But I do hope you will talk with her and hear her side of things. Give her another chance when you can and see what happens.

"I don't know if I can, but I'll think about it."

"Good." She patted his hand and stood up. "Now, I'd better get the soup on, because I'll have a hungry crowd before long. And you, young man, need to get home."

He appreciated her attempt to lighten the mood. "I know when I'm being shooed out the door."

When he got home, instead of going directly inside, he walked around back to the shed. Marie no longer expected him to come straight inside, and he needed to do some thinking. And praying. Was Mom's advice what God had been telling him all along?

He knew he wasn't ready to brush it all behind him and start over now. With the pain he still felt, he couldn't. But he could work toward that end down the road. It would be a process, a journey, but it wouldn't happen if he didn't take one step in that direction.

Chapter Twenty-Two: Running Scared

After he'd spent some time in prayer and reflection, Oliver turned on the radio. He'd found it thrown back in a corner and cleaned it up, but it had definitely seen its better days. It only got one clear station, although a few others would come in sporadically.

The song by Roy Orbison that he'd heard back around the time when he'd first proposed to Marie filled the air.

> *Just runnin' scared each place we go*
> *So afraid that he might show*
> *Yeah, runnin' scared, what would I do*
> *If he came back and wanted you.*

He hurriedly turned it off. He remembered thinking back when he heard it in the truck that day months ago how that would never happen to him because Marie would never put him in that position. Had he really been that sure, and had he been sure of himself, Marie, or both? He felt as if he'd aged a hundred years since that day.

Had he really thought she would fall in love with him once she got to know him? Had he been that self-assured. She had tried to tell him it would never happen, but he'd thought she'd change her mind. Maybe he had set himself up for a hard fall.

He shook his head at himself. After all the verbal harassment he'd endured, how could he have thought such a thing? Marie had felt forced to marry him, but that didn't mean she would have chosen him for her husband over everyone else otherwise. He needed to face the fact that if she hadn't been pregnant, she would never have agreed to their wedding.

But beating himself up over the past wouldn't help a thing because he couldn't change the past. He needed to decide what he needed to do about the present. He needed to consider what would be best for all three of them om the future.

Mother had been right about his wedding vows? Made before God, they were to be taken seriously.

He didn't know what Marie needed and what would be best for her, but from what he knew of the guy, he doubted it would be Derrick. He had manipulated and used Marie and wanted to continue doing so. He heard his teeth grind and tried to clear his mind from thinking about the jerk.

Davy needed a family, a father and mother who would love him. It seemed for the immediate future, Oliver needed to stay the course and see where it led, but he had never been more frightened about what the future might hold.

He also needed to be better behaved with Marie.

He wasn't ready to forgive her yet, but he hoped he could soon, and he needed to hear what she wanted to say. He felt too tired and haggard to do that tonight, but maybe tomorrow or Saturday.

Marie came out of the bedroom when she heard him come in. "Are there some sandwich fixings in here?" He opened the refrigerator.

He could feel her surprise that he'd initiated a conversation. There's peanut butter and jelly or some soup I can warm up if you'd rather have that."

"What kind of soup?"

"Homemade chicken noodle."

"That sounds good if it's not too much trouble, or I can heat it."

"No, let me get it. You sit down." She nodded toward the table and busied herself around the kitchen. She appeared eager to do something for him, and his heart softened a tiny bit.

She sat everything before him and looked unsure about what to do. "I've already eaten what I could. I have to try to eat a little, so I can nurse Davy."

"Have a seat." He kept his eyes on his soup bowl but heard the chair scrape as she pulled it out and sat down.

"Oliver, I hate his coldness between us. Is there anything we can do to make things any better?"

He looked at her. Her eyes glistened with unshed tears. "I honestly don't know, but we can try, I guess. I'm tired tonight, but I'll let you have your say soon. I'll try to come straight home tomorrow, and maybe we can talk after supper. If that doesn't work out, then we'll talk Saturday morning."

"You're going to eat supper here after work." Her voice held so much hope, he almost got strangled.

"If that's okay. It doesn't have to be anything big or elaborate. I still don't have much of an appetite."

She lowered her eyes. "Okay." Her voice became strained again at his reminder of the hurt she'd caused. "Thank you," she added a little later as she got up. "I'll just go check on Davy. Leave the things on the table and I'll be back to take care of them."

He poured the rest of his soup back in the container, cleaned up the table, and washed his few dishes. Marie shouldn't feel she needed to wait on him.

As he went to his room to get ready for bed, he noticed a difference. He didn't feel the same level of bitterness as before, and his burdens had lightened some. One step taken. Now, how many more would be needed, and would he ever get to a good place? Only God could know the future.

Oliver tried his best to listen to Marie objectively as she explained what had happened from her point of view, but he couldn't. He couldn't keep his rogue emotions from coloring everything.

"Even if you went to let him see Davy, I don't understand why you would let him kiss you. You are my wife, Marie. You married me. You shouldn't be kissing another man."

"No, I shouldn't." He could hear the desperation in her voice. "It was a mistake, a horrible mistake. I told myself I wanted to see how much it would still affect me because I knew I had begun to see some of Derrick's bad side, but I never should have allowed it. If I had it to do over, I would not go to meet him at all."

"And did his kiss still affect you?"

She jerked back, apparently not expecting that question. "I g-guess. A little but not nearly as much as it once would have. And not as much as your passionate ones have." Her voice had lowered on the last part.

He studied her. His mother had been right because he could tell Marie wanted to remain truthful. That made him feel some better, but what man wanted to hear that his wife liked the kisses of another man, even if not quite as much as before.

She looked at him with uncertain hope. "I can promise you that nothing like this will ever happen again. If I even see Derrick at a distance, I will let you know, and I will never agree to meet him again. I have learned a hard but needed lesson."

"I will try to accept that, but I don't know if I

can ever trust you again in the same way I used to."

"Maybe with time, I can earn that trust back."
She sounded defeated, and his heart felt caught in a
vise. With sudden clarity, he realized he still loved this
woman. She had betrayed him and hurt him beyond
words, but he still loved her. Love must be more
powerful than he realized.

But love didn't equal trust and happiness.
Hosea must have loved Gomer, but their marriage was
not a happy one.

Oliver cleared his throat. "In the meantime, I
will quit trying to avoid you and work to make our
relationship as comfortable as possible. However, it
may take time."

She nodded, and he saw her eyes glisten with
moisture again. "Thank you for listening. I will do
everything I can to make things better."

Marie turned on the radio as they rode to church
Sunday morning. The second verse of Roy Orbison's
hit played before she reached over and turned it off.

> *Just runnin' scared, feelin' low*
> *Runnin' scared, you love him so*
> *Just runnin' scared afraid to lose*
> *If he came back which one would you choose*

"I keep hearing that blasted song way too

much." He looked at her to see what her reaction would be.

"I don't like the song anymore, but I hope you know it doesn't apply to us. I don't love Derrick so, for one thing."

"No?" He wanted to also ask if Derrick came back and wanted her, which one would she choose, but he feared the answer. He had taken a couple more steps forward, and he needed some time before taking another.

"How are you two doing? His mom asked as they walked into the house after the service. They hadn't a chance to say much at church. She sounded casual, as if she were asking about their welfare like she had done hundreds of times, but Oliver knew what she meant.

"We're doing some better, I guess." By the look on her face, his answer created more questions, but she nodded and busied herself putting the meal on the table.

He and Marie must have acted close to normal around the table, because everyone seemed to relax, and no one stared at them. They still weren't close or as comfortable in each other's presence as they had been, but he had buried his animosity and bitterness, and that had made things easier.

Lord, help me to do what is right, regardless of

my hurt and pain. I fear I have suddenly become too self-centered over what Marie did. The pain had driven me inward. Help me consider Davy's and her welfare above my own. Help me follow your will, I pray. Amen.

Chapter Twenty-Three: An Unexpected End

Marie glanced at Oliver as she helped his mother set the table. She knew he was saying a silent prayer, and her heart went out to him. He had been trying not to hold a grudge against her, but she knew it must be hard. She didn't know how she'd feel to learn that he had been meeting and kissing another woman.

She couldn't imagine how she'd feel, because she knew she didn't have to worry about Oliver doing such a thing. She could trust him without question. Oh, how she wished he could say the same thing about her.

A part of her wanted to blame Derrick for everything, but she couldn't. Sure, he'd played a part, but he had never forced her to do anything. She had made her own choices.

"You've made your own bed, now lay in it," her daddy would say. You'd think to hear him, he'd never made a mistake, but she knew better.

Sunday dinner went well, and Oliver even smiled a couple of times. Although weaker than before, it did her heart good to see his dimple pop out. She and he each had just one.

Davy got fussy and Marie wanted to go home, feed him, and put him down for a nap. The family had passed him around enough that they'd tired him out with all the attention.

Maybe she and Oliver could get an afternoon nap, too. Not together, of course. Oliver wouldn't want that now, and neither would she. They needed to work through more of their issues before they arrived at that point.

Each day seemed a little lighter and a little brighter as if another speck of grime had been wiped away. She spent extra time cooking, cleaning, and doing laundry to try to make things extra nice for Oliver. But she had to be careful not to push him. She found when she did, he retreated. No, better let him set the pace. At least things were headed in the right direction, even if they were excruciatingly slow.

Spring came, the trees started putting out tiny green leaves, flowers budded with a burst of sudden color, and the world held the promise of new life. Marie tried not to get her hopes up, but she wanted so much for things to be right between her and Oliver again.

They had made progress and the tensions had mostly eased. However, he had never intentionally touched her again – never held her hand, never put his hand on the small of her back, and certainly never kissed her, not even on the cheek or forehead.

She had hoped they could talk things out and that would enable them to put her past failures behind them, but that was not to be. Oliver had grown kinder with her, but he held back showing any feelings. Did he even have any feelings for her anymore, or had she killed them in all her foolishness?

As much as she wanted to let her hope spring forth with the season, she found herself in moments of depression. She wished she could quit worrying and let the future take care of itself, but her impatience made that nearly impossible. If she just had the answers to her most pressing questions, but she didn't think she should ask them. Did Oliver still love her as he'd once said that he did? Did he still want her for his wife? Could he ever completely forgive her and be happy with her?

Friday began like any other, but Oliver came home before noon. "I have a horrible headache, and pain relievers haven't helped. Mr. Little sent me home." His eyes looked weak and strained, and she could almost feel his pain.

"Do you need to go to the doctor?" She worried because Oliver had never gotten sick.

He started to shake his head but stopped. The pain must be intense indeed. "I've taken some aspirin. I'll just go lie down."

"I'll come in a check on you in a few minutes." She'd give him time to get into bed first.

When she went to check on him, he had his

eyes closed, but he opened them when she entered the room. She put her hand on his forehead, and he tensed as if he wished he could knock it away. "You don't feel as if you have a fever, but would a cool, damp washcloth make you feel better?"

"I don't know." He shut his eyes again. "I don't guess it would hurt to see."

She dampened a washcloth and quietly placed it on his forehead. His eyes flickered open. "Thank you. Marie…." His voice had softened more than she had heard it lately, but they both paused when they heard a car pull up.

She went to the window, since this bedroom faced the front, and her heart fell to her toes. "Derrick. Now, what does he want?" She sure didn't want to see him. He'd caused enough trouble.

Oliver sat up, wide-eyed. "Did you say Derrick?" He swung his legs off the bed and grabbed his pants.

Marie went toward the front door, knowing that Oliver would soon follow. Derrick hopped out of his Corvette and leaned against it, expecting her to come to him. She didn't. She stopped a little off the porch. "What do you want now?" She knew her voice sounded none too friendly.

"What do I always want, Baby? You, I always want you."

"You've ruined things enough. Go away."

Marie felt Oliver come up beside her, and she saw Derrick pale. "I-I thought he'd be at work."

"I'm sure you did." Her voice hardened with disdain. "You'd rather sneak around behind his back."

Derrick's eyes locked back on her as if he chose to ignore Oliver. "I had to make one more attempt to see you, to convince you to come away with me."

She heard Oliver's intake of breath, but she needed to make Derrick leave as soon as possible, so she kept her focus on him. "Come away with you?"

"You win, Marie. I'll marry you. You can even bring the kid if you want, and we can be a family. I'm sure Oliver won't contest your divorce."

She grew weak from the shock. Had Derrick really decided he wanted to marry her? Maybe she should consider it since things might never be right between her and Oliver again. "You want to marry me?"

"Yeah. I'm sorry I have to ask like this. I know it's not very romantic. I'm also sorry it took me this long to come to my senses. I guess I just didn't know how much I was going to miss you. I promise I'll make it up to you. Say yes, Baby. Say you'll come with me right now." Derrick's voice wrapped around her like a warm blanket, soft and soothing.

Oliver clenched his fists at his side and stared at his nemesis across the yard. The man exuded confidence and a self-assuredness that said he always got what he wanted.

Derrick stepped away from the shiny red sports car and took a step toward Marie. "Come on, honey. You know we were meant to be together. I love you."

This was it. The moment Oliver had been afraid of for weeks now. Given the choice, he had no doubts which one Marie would choose. Her previous actions had proven it. His wife, the woman he still loved, would crawl into the red Corvette with the little boy he thought of as a son and ride out of his life forever. And he had himself to blame, at least in part. He hadn't been the easiest man to live with lately, and he hadn't treated her as he should.

He should have forgiven her sooner and shown her how much he still loved her. Instead, he had pushed her away and kept her at arms' length. By being afraid to trust her, he had lost her forever.

He wanted to take her hand and beg her to stay, but he felt like a lead statue that couldn't move. His tongue had grown so thick and his throat so dry, he didn't think he could utter a single sound. It wouldn't do any good anyway. He could beg until he was blue in the face, and she would still choose Derrick. It had always been Derrick.

"I'll still go to college, but we can get an apartment. With a wife, a kid, and school, I shouldn't have to go in the army anytime soon." Derrick opened his car door and gestured for Marie to come get in. The last verse of that cursed song was playing on his radio.

Then all at once he was standing there
So sure of himself, his head in the air
My heart was breaking, which one would it be

Derrick shut the door and walked toward Marie as if he were going to take her hand and pull her to the car. Oliver acted without thinking. His right fist came up and slammed into the jerk's face. Derrick toppled to the ground.

Oliver felt Marie jerk beside him as if he had hit her. "I'm not going to apologize." He knew it wouldn't make any difference, but he felt he'd done something to show what he thought of the man.

He expected Marie to rush to Derrick's side, but she turned to Oliver, and her eyes searched his. He lowered his guard for the first time since Annie's announcement and hoped she could read what his mouth couldn't get out.

She turned back to Derrick who had almost struggled back to his feet. For a moment, Oliver thought she would go help steady him and lead him back to his car, but she didn't. Instead, she sided closer to Oliver and took one of his hands. He unclenched his fist and laced his fingers through hers.

His heart almost broke all over again when she turned back toward Derrick, but her words were almost unbelievable. "I would never choose you over my husband, Derrick. You only care about pleasing yourself. Oliver wants to please me, and I love him more than I thought possible.

Derrick grew pale and his eyes widened as if he couldn't believe what he heard. He started to say something, but then tightened his lips. He stared at Marie, then turned, walked slowly back to the Corvette, and left.

"You turned around and walked away with me," Oliver sang the last line of the song he now knew by heart, wonder filling his heart.

A wide grin spread across Marie's face. "Yes, I did, didn't I? Can we start over?"

"No." When her face fell, he hurried to explain. "We'll put the past in the past, but we won't start over. That's too far to go back. We'll start from today, better and stronger than ever before."

"I like how you think, Mr. Hartsell. In fact, I like everything about you. I love you more than words can say."

I love you, too," he told her before he encircled her in his arms and spun her off the ground in joy. Her laughter bubbled over.

He let her down easy, feeling a little dizzy from their twirl. He kissed her slowly and passionately, letting all his pent-up emotions out, saying things words could never express. She returned his kiss as never before.

He kept his arm around her when it ended, and they turned to go inside. She stayed close to him and he kept his arm around her.

"Perhaps we should take those steaks out of the freezer for supper tonight." She looked at him with other questions in her eyes.

Did she mean what he thought? "I'd like that. I'd like that very much." He could hardly wait, in fact.

"How's your headache?"

"I do believe it's gone." He opened and closed the front door quietly, so as not to awake Davy as they went inside.

"Could you still use a nap? Since Davy is sleeping in my room, and I don't want to disturb him, perhaps I could join you."

There was no mistaking what she meant by that. "I'd love for you to join me." If that kiss had been any indication, their lives were about to get a whole lot better, and they'd have a lifetime to enjoy each other